Bringing Them Home

BARBARA HINSKE

Also by BARBARA HINSKE:
Coming to Rosemont, the first novel in the *Rosemont* series
Weaving the Strands, the second novel in the *Rosemont* series
Uncovering Secrets, the third novel in the *Rosemont* series
Drawing Close, the fourth novel in the *Rosemont* series
The Night Train
The Christmas Club
Available at Amazon and for Kindle.

I'd love to hear from you! Connect with me online:
Visit **www.barbarahinske.com** and sign up
for my **newsletter** to receive your Free Gift, plus Inside Scoops, Amazing Offers,
Bedtime Stories & Inspirations from Home.
Facebook.com/BHinske
Twitter.com/BarbaraHinske
Search for **Barbara Hinske on YouTube** for tours inside my own
historic home plus tips and tricks for busy women!
Find photos of fictional *Rosemont,* Westbury, and things related to the *Rosemont*
series at **Pinterest.com/BarbaraHinske**.
bhinske@gmail.com

Library of Congress Control Number: 2017933656
ISBN-13: 978-0-9962747-5-3
ISBN-10: 0-9962747-5-8

Casa del Northern Publishing
Phoenix, Arizona

Dedication

To my loyal and engaged readers whose kind encouragement, enthusiasm, and support have made my author journey a joy.

Chapter 1

Chuck Delgado yanked the cord on the mini blinds and opened his office window to the moonless night. The faint smell of gasoline from the row of gas pumps below wafted up to him on the second floor. His store below had closed an hour earlier, and he now had the place to himself.

Delgado raised the bottle of Jameson to his lips and took a long drink. He set the bottle on the windowsill and stared into the darkness.

Out there—somewhere—someone was trying to make sure that he was the only one charged with fraud and embezzlement against the Town of Westbury. He—Chuck Delgado—was going to be the patsy. He slammed his fist on the sill, sending the bottle of whiskey to the floor. It shattered into pieces at his feet, the pungent amber liquid seeping into the carpet.

Delgado cursed loudly and retraced his steps to his desk. He dropped into his chair, leaned back, and closed his eyes. His lawyer assured him that the state's case was weak, that there was no way he would be convicted of any crime. He wasn't so sure.

Delgado ripped open his desk drawer and rummaged for a pen and piece of paper. It was time to make a list of the people who had betrayed him. He'd deal with them if his attorney's confidence proved to be unfounded. If he needed to take matters into his own hands, he'd be ready.

Delgado wrote the first entry on the list: Maggie Martin. That do-gooder mayor was the one who'd turned the Town of Westbury against him. He paused for an instant, then smiled mirthlessly and resumed his task.

Chapter 2

Maggie Martin opened the back door of Rosemont and ushered the two men on her doorstep into the comforting warmth of the kitchen. The dogs abandoned their beds to welcome the visitors. "Thanks for coming on short notice, Sam," she said, hugging the older man. Sam Torres was one of her first and dearest friends in Westbury. "You too, David. John and I are so glad you're here."

David Wheeler nodded and held out his arms to Roman as the golden retriever made a beeline for him.

"Anything to help," Sam replied, dropping to one knee to greet the terrier mix. Eve rested her front paws on his leg while she tried to lick his face. "We want everything to be ready when Susan comes home from the hospital. Joan and I are so happy she's getting better. We've been praying for her."

Maggie took a deep breath. "Thank you, Sam. I knew these superbugs could be serious, but I had no idea how quickly they moved and how sick she'd become. We almost lost her."

"And after doing such a noble thing—donating a kidney to her half-sister." Sam shook his head as he stood and patted Maggie's arm. "But she survived, and now she's coming home. So, what can we do to help?"

"Can you equip the bathroom by the conservatory with grab bars and anything else you think it might need? I'm not sure if she'll be able to handle the stairs, so John and Aaron moved a bed down here," she said, walking them into the conservatory.

"Good thinking," Sam said. "This room's got plenty of light and the view of the back garden is spectacular, even with the snow."

"Aaron will be here the rest of the week to help her, but then he has to return to his residency in California."

"What a way to start a marriage," Sam said. "A honeymoon *and* their first Christmas together in the hospital? I tell you, it can only get better from here."

"I agree. But if they can get through this, I think they can get through anything together." Maggie turned to David. "Glenn Vaughn tells me you and Dodger are spending a lot of time at Fairview Terraces, bringing pet therapy to the elderly. I'd like you to have a good look around—tell me if there's anything we need to do to make it safe for Susan. She's still a little weak and will probably be in a wheelchair for most of the first week. I'd like to make her transition here as smooth as possible."

David nodded. "I've noticed lots of little things there, like they don't have throw rugs and all of the electrical cords are fastened out of the way. I'll make sure that it's all set for her."

"When do you expect her home?" Sam asked.

"Tomorrow or the day after." Maggie sighed heavily and pushed her thick brown hair off her face. "It can't be soon enough."

"We'd better get busy." He turned to his teenage helper. "We'll stay until everything's been done."

David nodded his agreement.

"Alex is on his way over. We'll be working in the library if you need me for anything." Maggie started down the hall, then turned back. "John's headed to Tomascino's to pick up a couple of pizzas. He's bringing back plenty for all of us, so feel free to help yourselves."

David grinned.

"And he said he's getting extra pepperoncini for you, David."

Maggie set the plate holding her half-eaten slice of pizza on the library desk and leaned over to reexamine the two sets of spreadsheets.

"We've been over these countless times," Alex said. "There's just not enough here. And we're set for trial in less than three months. The state has to prove its case against Delgado—or he walks. Based upon this," he said, sweeping his arm over the desk, "we not only *won't* get a conviction, we'll be the laughing stock of the town. The press will have a field day with us."

"I'm sure it won't be that bad," John interjected. He leaned against the mantel over the tall stone fireplace, arms crossed over his chest. "I'm a veterinarian not a lawyer, so I can't comment on the sufficiency of the evidence." He pointed to the spreadsheets. "But the people of Westbury know how hard you've worked and how sleazy Delgado is. Anyone who's lived here long enough has heard the rumors of his mob connections. If you don't get a conviction, the public will be disappointed but they won't laugh at you."

Alex ran both hands through his hair. "John—with all due respect—I think you're wrong. If this trial goes the way I think it will, I'll be reduced to chasing ambulances, and your wife, here," he pointed to Maggie, "won't have a prayer of being re-elected mayor of Westbury."

"That's the least of my worries," Maggie said. "My concern—my *only* concern—is making Delgado pay for abusing his seat on the town council by embezzling money from the town's general fund and the town workers' pension fund." She stood and faced both men. "Alex is right; we don't have enough. There has to be a third spreadsheet out there—William Wheeler was meticulous in recording these accounts. David and I missed it when we went through their house on the night before the foreclosure. I still can't believe we forgot to check the garage. It must have been hidden in there."

"And since the baseboards—which is where David found these two—" Alex lifted the spreadsheets and flung them back on the table, "were ripped out of the garage before the police got there, no doubt Delgado has it now. These two link the offshore accounts to the embezzled town funds, but we need to get our hands on that third spreadsheet. It's got to list the bank accounts the embezzled funds were wired to. The owners of these accounts need to go to jail."

"Delgado bought the house at the foreclosure sale, so he's the most likely person to have it," John said. "Maybe you should get a warrant to search his office?"

"You think I haven't thought of that?" Alex rounded on John. "It's not that simple. A judge has to issue the warrant, and so far, the judge feels that we've searched Delgado enough. Says we don't need another 'fishing expedition.'"

"Then we need to find another way," Maggie said, calmly placing her hand on Alex's shoulder. "I don't know how, but we're going to get that spreadsheet."

David Wheeler crossed the living room, headed for the kitchen and another slice of pizza. Blossom and Buttercup chased each other at the end of the hallway, and he headed in the cats' direction. He had a fondness for the littermates of his cat, Namor. Buttercup leapt into his arms while Blossom rubbed against his legs. David paused outside the library, petting the cat as she purred. He heard raised voices and inched closer to the door.

When Mayor Martin had told them she was meeting with Special Counsel Scanlon, David knew it had to be about the case against Chuck Delgado—the sleazeball who had involved David's father in the fraud and embezzlement scheme. His father had been forced to resign his seat as mayor and had gone to jail—where he'd taken his own life.

David felt the blood pounding in his ears, as he always did when he thought of his dad and the fate that had befallen him. What had happened to the easygoing, fun-loving father that he'd known? The *Westbury Gazette* was wrong; his dad wasn't a crook or a mobster.

David held his breath as he listened at the library door. He could hear them perfectly. He nodded in agreement. The two spreadsheets he'd found weren't enough. But his dad would have made a third spreadsheet, and that third spreadsheet must be in Chuck Delgado's possession. David had to find it.

Chapter 3

With Dodger at his side, David stepped onto the elevator and pushed the button for the children's ward. The one-eyed therapy dog was a hit everywhere they went and was a particular favorite with the kids at Mercy Hospital. As the elevator went up, David wondered whether Dodger's traumatic past had given his dog heightened empathetic powers.

When David adopted him, Dodger was already missing an eye, which Dr. Allen suspected was the result of an illegal dog fight. Then last year during an agility training course, Dodger dislocated a shoulder, tore some ligaments, and had to have emergency surgery. Normally, the injuries would make a dog hesitant to be around people—especially small children who showed their love with repetitive head pats, choke-inducing hugs, and sticky kisses. But Dodger never seemed to tire of their affection.

The elevator stopped and the pair made their way to the nurses' station. David recognized the matronly woman sitting behind a computer monitor, stabbing at her keyboard, and scowling at the screen. She looked up as the two approached and a smile quickly replaced her frown.

"Hi, David. Nice to see you. How's my boy, Dodger?" she asked, rising and coming around to the front of the workstation. She knelt and greeted the dog who wagged his tail politely.

"Were you having trouble with your computer?" David asked.

"When am I not?" She sighed. "We've got the slowest system in the Western world. Drives me crazy." She glanced up at David. "I'm glad to see you. Someone was just asking for you."

"Really? Who?"

"Nicole Nash," the nurse said.

David frowned and took a step back.

"She's doing just fine," the nurse added hastily. "I didn't mean to alarm you. She's here for some follow-up testing—and everything looks good."

David released the breath he'd been holding.

"She's been up to the nurses' station twice to ask about you." She pointed toward the community playroom at the end of wing. "I think she's in there."

David nodded and signaled for Dodger to follow him.

"Stop back here to see me before the two of you leave, okay?" she called after them. "You always make my day."

―――――

"Here he is!" the four-year-old squealed and raced across the busy playroom to throw her arms around the dog's neck. Dodger patiently accepted her attention.

"How are you today, Miss Nicole?" David asked.

"Not sick anymore," Nicole tipped her shining face up to look at him. "My sister gave me a real good kidney. I'm all better."

"I'm glad to hear that," David said.

"I wanted to tell Dodger that I'm fine," Nicole said. "And I want him to meet Tommy."

"Sure." David scanned the room. "Is he in here?"

Nicole shook her head. "He doesn't feel well enough to come play. That's why Dodger needs to see him. To help him feel happy." She nodded her head knowingly. "He helped me feel happy when I hurt."

David looked away and swallowed the lump in his throat. "Then we'd better go find Tommy. Can you take us to him?"

Nicole put her hand on Dodger's leash and led them to a room on the other side of the corridor. A pretty girl with waist-length strawberry blond hair and large green eyes came to the door.

"Come in," she said, her smile brightening when she saw Dodger. "My brother's been looking forward to meeting this guy."

The room opened to a maze of wires and tubes that linked a small boy to several pieces of beeping equipment. He faced the ceiling, but David could see a large bandage covered his left eye. Dodger gently nudged the boy's arm with his nose, and Nicole giggled.

"Tommy, this is Dodger," Nicole said, then leaned in and whispered. "He's the one I told you about."

A faint smile crossed Tommy's lips. He raised a hand and placed it on top of Dodger's head. "Can I pet him?"

"Of course," David replied, trying to keep his attention on Tommy instead of his very attractive sister. He wondered how old she was and where she went to school. "Dodger loves attention."

"Is he in the hospital, too?" Tommy asked, pointing to Dodger's missing eye.

"No. He lives with me. He's gotten better from his injury."

"I had a tumor and they had to operate," Tommy said. "I'm going to be all right, too."

"Glad to hear it," David said. "Do you want me to raise the head of your bed, so you can see him better?"

"No," his sister said quickly. "He needs to lie flat until tomorrow morning." She knelt down to greet Dodger. "My name's Grace, by the way," she said, looking at David.

"I'm David Wheeler. How did you know about Dodger?"

"Nicole told me about him when we met in the playroom. I went in search of a book to read to Tommy. We have a dog at home, and I knew Tommy would want a visit from Dodger." David watched in fascination as she gathered her hair with one hand and twirled it into a coil that she knotted at the nape of her neck.

"We'll be back tomorrow," David said. "Would you like us to come see you again?"

Tommy's face lit up.

"That's really nice of you," Grace said, turning her emerald eyes to him.

"I'll come after school." He cleared his throat. "Do you go to Westbury High?"

"I'm starting there, day after tomorrow. My family just moved here, for my dad's job. He's a professor at Highpointe. They're signing papers for our new house right now."

"That's good," he said, his heart beating wildly in his chest. "I'm a junior. What grade are you in?"

"I should be a senior, but we lived in Hungary for two years and not all of my credits transferred, so I'll be a junior, too."

"Maybe we'll have some classes together." David shifted his weight from foot to foot. "If you need anything, you can always ask me."

Her smile rocked him back on his heels. "I may take you up on that. See you tomorrow." She turned to her brother who was sleeping with one hand on Dodger's head.

David nodded and reluctantly steered Dodger toward the door. "Come on, Miss Nicole. Tommy needs to sleep. Why don't you take me to see some of the other kids?"

With Nicole leading the way, David and Dodger exited the room before David could see the admiring look on Grace's face as she watched him go.

Chapter 4

Maggie snatched her coat from the back of her office door and rushed past her assistant's desk. "Susan's been released, and I'm going to pick her up. Call or text if you need me."

The woman smiled and shooed Maggie toward the elevator. "Don't worry about anything—and don't even *think* about coming back to the office today. Just go get your girl."

Maggie hurried to the elevator. John was busy at Westbury Animal Hospital, so she dashed off a short text with the good news as she rode to the first floor. Aaron had told her to meet them at the entrance to Mercy Hospital. He'd be with Susan when they brought her downstairs in a wheelchair.

Maggie pulled to the curb slightly in front of the entrance and put the car in park. The January day was sunny and clear, but the reading on her dashboard thermometer convinced her to keep the engine running and the heater on while she waited for her daughter and new son-in-law. Maggie turned and fixed her gaze on the entrance.

She started when someone knocked on her driver's side window, and spun around to see David Wheeler standing outside.

"I didn't mean to startle you, ma'am," he said, as she opened the window. "I just wanted to see if everything's all right."

"It's better than all right." She beamed. "Susan's been released, and Aaron will be bringing her to the car any minute now. We're taking her home to Rosemont."

"That's great news. Be sure to call Sam or me if you need us to do anything else for you. We'll come right away."

"I know you will, David. Thank you. I think the two of you thought of everything we'll need for Susan. We're all set." Maggie leaned out the window and looked down at the dog sitting obediently at his feet. "How are the two of you doing? You're still coming to the hospital after school?"

"Only one day a week. Yesterday was our regular day, but we're back today to see one particular patient. We think he needs some extra attention."

Maggie smiled at his use of the word "we." David and Dodger shared the seamless bond of affection and acceptance that she knew could happen between a dog and its owner. "That's very nice of you—both of you," Maggie replied. She glanced over her shoulder at the entrance just as the electronic doors opened and her tall, dark-haired son-in-law wheeled Susan onto the sidewalk. "They're here!" she cried, as David opened her car door.

Maggie hurried around the back of her car. "Let's get you inside before you catch a cold," Maggie said to her daughter, dropping a kiss onto her cheek.

"I've got my coat on, Mom. I'm fine." Susan squeezed her mother's hand and turned to David. "Hello, David," Susan called, then snapped her fingers and gestured to Dodger to come to her. The dog and his owner obliged.

Susan ruffled Dodger's ears. "I heard the two of you were coming today to see that boy who's had eye surgery"—she smiled up at David—"and that this boy has a very pretty older sister who will be in your grade at school."

David blushed and looked aside. "Who told you that?"

"Nicole came to see me yesterday afternoon when she was done with her tests."

David shrugged. "His sister seemed nice enough ..."

Susan winked at her mother and Aaron.

"All right, sweetheart." Aaron smiled at his mischievous wife. "You'll have to finish giving David the third degree another time," he said, pointing to the line of cars behind them. "I need to help m'lady into her chariot, so we can get out of the way." He held his hand out to Susan.

"We need to get going, too. C'mon, boy," David said, eager to be out of Susan's crosshairs. "I'll see you around!" He waved goodbye over his shoulder as he and Dodger made a break for the hospital.

"Good luck with the girl," Susan called as Aaron helped her out of her wheelchair and into Maggie's car.

<hr />

David crossed the lobby in long strides and waited impatiently for the elevator. Despite the teasing he'd just endured, he had to admit he was looking forward to seeing Grace again. He waved at the nurse he'd talked to the day before and went directly to Tommy's room.

David's knock on the door frame was answered by a hearty "come in" in a mature man's voice. David entered the room cautiously, but Dodger went straight to the bed in the center of the room, where Tommy was sitting up, eating pudding, and watching a cartoon. The large bandage had been replaced by a small gauze square held in place by an eye patch.

"Hi, Tommy," David said as Dodger laid his muzzle on the bed. Tommy greeted Dodger with pudding-covered hands.

David smiled and turned to the couple standing on the other side of Tommy's bed. "Hi, I'm David."

"We're Iris and Kevin Acosta," the man said. "We're Tommy's parents."

"Grace told us all about the two of you," Iris said.

David felt butterflies in his stomach at the mention of Grace's name.

"Tommy's been so excited about seeing Dodger today," she continued. "And you, of course," she hastened to add.

David looked at Tommy. "Dodger was ready to go the minute I got home from school. He knew we were coming back to see you."

Tommy grinned. "Dogs know when you like them," he said as he leaned over and threw his arms around Dodger's neck.

"How's Tommy doing?" David asked.

"He's coming along nicely," Iris said. "He's healing ahead of schedule, and the doctors are hopeful that this surgery has solved the problem. The tumor was benign, thank God." She rubbed her son's back. "He's been through so many surgeries."

The three of them watched as the boy stroked Dodger's silky ears, an expression of complete happiness on Tommy's face.

"Being with Dodger is doing more to help him than anything else at this point," Iris said quietly. "I tried to get permission to bring our dog in from home, but they wouldn't grant it," she said with a sigh.

"When do you expect him to be released?"

"In the next couple of days," Iris said.

"Why don't I come back every day this week after school until Tommy goes home?"

"That would be so kind of you," she said, bringing her hands together to her chest.

"Are you sure you have time, son?" Kevin asked.

David nodded emphatically.

"You can come with me after school." Grace entered the room, carrying three Styrofoam cups. "I just went for coffee," she said as she flashed a smile at David. "Do you like macchiatos?" She pulled a cup out of the paper carrier and extended it to him. "Here. You can have mine."

David shook his head. "I'm fine, thank you."

"Grace is starting school tomorrow, and I'm going to pick her up by the office when classes are over. Why don't you meet us there, and we'll swing by your house to get Dodger?" Kevin asked. "I'll drive you back home when we're done. That'll save you gas money, too."

"I don't have a car," David said. "I take the bus here."

"Then it's settled," Kevin said. "We'll see you tomorrow afternoon. You can answer any questions Grace has about the school on the way here. She told us about your offer to help her out."

David felt a flush creep up his neck. Why was he so pleased that Grace had spoken to her parents about him? He snuck a quick glance at Grace, who was smiling at him. "That'll work. See you tomorrow."

Susan placed her elbows on the large farmhouse table in Rosemont's breakfast room and cradled her head in her hands. "I don't know if it's because I stuffed myself with Pete's wonderful pot roast," she said, nodding to the empty plate in front of her, "or whether I just don't have any stamina anymore, but I can hardly keep my eyes open." She turned to Aaron. "You can stay up, but I need to go to bed."

"I think we're all bushed," John said, rising from the table and picking up their plates. "You two go on ahead. Your mother and I will clean up the kitchen. Then I'm hitting the hay, too."

Aaron stood and began collecting the glassware from the table.

"Leave all that," Maggie said. "John's right. Since you're going back to your surgical residency in California tomorrow and you just got out of the hospital, you two should spend time together—not with us clearing the table."

"Thanks, Mom," Susan said, taking Aaron's hand and pulling herself to her feet. "And speaking of that, I'm going to sleep upstairs tonight."

"But we've got everything all ready for you in the conservatory. John and Aaron brought the twin bed down for you, and Sam and David outfitted the bathroom with grab bars and safety features."

Susan looked at Maggie and smiled weakly. "I know, Mom, and I appreciate everything you've done for me, for us." She squeezed Aaron's hand. "I promise I'll stay in the conservatory after Aaron goes home tomorrow. But we haven't had one night alone since we got married. Aaron might have to drag me," she said, smiling up at her new husband, "but we're going up those stairs to my room tonight."

Maggie opened her mouth to protest, but John put his hand on her shoulder. "I'm sure you'll be fine with Aaron. You two go on now. I've scheduled myself in later tomorrow morning, so I can drive you to the airport, Aaron. What time do you want to leave here?"

"We should be on our way by five fifteen," Aaron said. "Thank you, John. I hate to take you away from your practice."

"It's no problem," John replied. "I've hired Neil Braxton, that young vet who took care of my practice while Maggie and I were on our honeymoon. He'll be there in the morning."

"Have a good night's sleep, you two." Maggie took Susan's face in her hands and kissed her on the forehead. "I'll be working at home tomorrow, so I'll be right here if you need me."

"That's not necessary, Mom. I'm fine now. And if anything happened, I'd call you."

Aaron put his arm around Susan's waist. "I agree that you'll be all right staying here alone, but if your mom can arrange her schedule, so she can spend a few days at home with you, I think it's a good idea."

"Oh, for heaven's sake—" Susan began, but Aaron cut her off.

"You gave all of us quite a scare, Susan. If we want to err on the side of caution, you're going to have to put up with it."

Susan raised her hands in defeat.

"I'll probably get more done here than I would at Town Hall. And Alex is coming by at two, so you'll be able to see him."

"That would be nice." Susan tried to stifle a yawn. "I'd like to talk to him."

Maggie inserted her hands into her rubber gloves. "You two scram, or we'll never get this kitchen cleaned up. You know me—I never go to bed until the kitchen is clean."

Aaron took the blood pressure cuff off of the top of the bureau and walked to the side of the bed where Susan sat smoothing lotion onto her hands and arms.

"Stop right there, Dr. Scanlon. You are not taking my blood pressure tonight." She shot him a stern glance. "Don't even think about taking my temperature."

"Come on, Susan, these are just common sense procedures."

"I agree. That's why I took them myself while you were getting ready for bed. I'm fine." She swung her feet under the covers and lay back against her pillow, smoothing her hair. "Tonight, I want you to be my husband and not my doctor." She patted the bed next to her. "This may not be the honeymoon we had in mind, but you're leaving tomorrow, and I want to make the most of the time we have tonight."

Aaron tossed the blood pressure cuff onto a chair and climbed into bed with his wife.

Susan turned onto her side and looked at the ornate tabletop clock. Sunshine streamed through the tall conservatory windows, bathing the table by her bed in warm light. It was two forty-five. She sat bolt upright. She hadn't meant to nap that long.

She'd gotten up early to see Aaron off. He and John insisted she stay and sleep in rather than accompany them on the drive to the airport. She'd turned on the television but found the daytime shows uninteresting and decided to take a nap. She was sleeping to relieve boredom—she needed something stimulating to focus on.

Alex should be here by now, and she wanted to see him. She had a plan.

Susan dislodged Bubbles from her perch, threw back the alpaca throw that Joan Torres had knitted for her while she was in the hospital, and swung her feet over the side of the bed. For the first time in days, she didn't need to pause to let the dizziness subside when she stood up. She slipped her feet into her slippers, ran a comb through her hair, and made a beeline for the library.

The door stood ajar and the room looked abandoned. Her mother's computer was on and her purse was on the floor by her desk. A pair of sunglasses and a set of keys lay on an end table. Her mother and Alex had to be around here somewhere.

She turned down the hall and the unmistakable smell of coffee and bacon enveloped her. Susan smiled. They were in the kitchen, of course. During all of Susan's formative years, the kitchen had been her mother's command center. Projects or problems were tackled at their kitchen table, surrounded by the aroma of comfort food and the sight of her mother deftly moving about her domain.

Susan pushed through the door to find Alex, apron tied over his oxford shirt, frying bacon while Maggie stood near the sink, washing tomatoes. Eve and Roman circled at Alex's feet, hoping for a dropped morsel of bacon.

"Look at the two of you," Susan said.

"Oh, sweetie, did we disturb you? You were taking a nap when I checked on you."

"No. I woke up on my own. And I'm glad I did. This smells fantastic."

"Doesn't it?" Maggie agreed. "Neither of us has eaten," she said, "and I had all of this bacon that needed to get used before it went bad." She smiled at Alex. "So here we are."

Alex wiped his hands on a towel and gave Susan a kiss on the cheek. "How's my favorite sister-in-law?"

"Other than being bored out of my mind, I'm absolutely great. Never been better."

"Glad to hear it—you could use a little boredom in your life after the weeks you've had," he replied. He removed the last slices of crispy bacon from the pan with a pair of tongs and laid them on a tray lined with paper towels.

"You've cooked that bacon perfectly," Susan said, snatching a piece. "Your talents never cease to amaze me."

"This may be my only marketable skill soon. Good to know I might have a future as a short order cook." He glanced at her. "You're going to join us, aren't you?"

"I'd never turn down a BLT."

Maggie handed Susan a bag of potato chips and a jug of iced tea. "Why don't you take these to the table, and we'll bring the sandwiches."

Susan raised an eyebrow at the chips.

"Don't judge," Maggie replied. "A BLT is best eaten with potato chips. I haven't let myself enjoy one of these in years, so I'm going to do it up right. Extra mayo and the whole bit."

"It almost seems like you're celebrating," Susan remarked as she moved to the table. "Are things going better with the Chuck Delgado case?"

"Things are going terribly. And even if we had the evidence we need, he's got a dozen lawyers to our two. They're burying us in motions and discovery requests," Alex replied. "We're so busy responding to them that we haven't had time to focus on the pleadings we want to file."

"Funny you should mention that," Susan said as Alex placed a plate with a BLT in front of her, and he and Maggie took their seats. "I meant it when I said I'm bored. I think I'll regain my stamina sooner if I have something intellectually stimulating to do."

"Have you tried sudoku, honey?" Maggie asked. "Or any of those brain teaser apps that you can get on your phone? Judy Young loves them."

Susan wrinkled her nose. "That's not what I have in mind, Mom." She looked at Alex. "I think we could help each other out. You need legal help and can't afford to pay for it, and I'm a bored lawyer who's on paid medical leave." She leaned back in her chair.

"Why don't I draft motions and write pleadings for you? I already know a lot about the facts of the case. You can email me papers to review and tell me how you'd like to respond. I can do any necessary research online and work right from my own bed. It's the perfect solution—for both of us. What do you say?"

"I'd say my brother married one heck of a gal. Are you sure you're well enough to take this on?" Alex asked.

"I am. And I'll be right here, so I can take breaks whenever I need them. You'd be doing me a favor."

"I don't buy that for an instant. But if you're sincere, I'm going to take you up on it." Alex turned to Maggie. "Are you okay with this—both as her mother and as the mayor?"

Maggie paused and looked between the two of them. She finally nodded.

"I'll send you a motion for summary judgment that we need to respond to by Monday. Can you handle that?"

Susan rolled her eyes. "You must be joking. I'm used to far tighter deadlines than that. Bring it on, Mr. Special Counsel."

Chapter 5

Frank Haynes approached the hostess at Stuart's Steakhouse shortly after they opened for dinner at five thirty. "Did you leave something here last night, Mr. Haynes?" the woman asked in a throaty voice shaped by decades of smoking.

Frank shook his head. "I enjoyed the special last night so much that I thought I'd come back."

The woman furrowed her brow. "It'll be something different tonight," she said, turning to point at the chalkboard behind her. "We've got sea bass or liver and onions."

"Perfect. I love them both. I'll have a hard time deciding."

The woman picked up a menu. "Dining alone again?"

Frank nodded.

"Right this way," she said and walked toward the bar.

Frank touched her elbow. "Would you mind if I sat in the same booth as last night?" he asked, pointing to the opposite corner of the restaurant. "The one on the far wall?"

"As you wish," she said, taking a sharp turn at the bar. He wondered why she seemed so annoyed with his request. He was the first patron in the restaurant; she could hardly refuse him.

"Thank you," Frank replied, forcing himself to be pleasant. What difference should it make to her where he sat or how many times he dined here? He was on a mission to have a private word with Chuck Delgado. With Delgado stripped of his town council seat, Frank had few opportunities to run into the man. He needed to speak to him—now—and couldn't risk being seen making a call on him. Delgado was a creature of habit, and Stuart's was his favorite restaurant. It was only a matter of time before he'd show up. In the meantime, Frank would eat his way through everything on the menu.

The table in the corner of the restaurant afforded him a clear view of all of the other diners. He was halfway through a shrimp cocktail when the familiar portly figure waddled into the restaurant, accompanied by his more refined brother.

23

Frank was more furious with Ron Delgado than with his thug of a brother. Some financial adviser Ron Delgado had been—counseling him to invest in offshore limited liability companies that loaned money to local businesses and sold the loans to the town workers' pension fund. How had he been so stupid as to think that he'd be helping the town while also making a hefty return on his investment?

Ron's recommendation had been unqualified, but he'd omitted the unsavory details of the investment scheme. Now Frank was up to his eyeballs in the fraud and embezzlement that had almost bankrupted the town. He'd made sure that the evidence pointed to Chuck Delgado; he'd even bribed an underworld figure in Miami to have his own name and account numbers removed from the records Special Counsel Scanlon had subpoenaed from the offshore banks. He'd stood silently by while Wheeler had been arrested, and felt responsible—at least in part—for the man's suicide. Frank couldn't allow anyone else to be hurt in connection with the whole fiasco.

Frank watched the brothers as they settled themselves at the bar. He was relieved when the bartender handed them each a menu; he didn't relish the idea of confronting Chuck Delgado after he'd had a liquid dinner. Frank finished the sea bass without tasting it and ordered a dessert he never intended to touch. He would linger at the table until the Delgado brothers were finished.

He was on his third cup of coffee when Ron Delgado signaled the bartender to bring their check. Chuck pried himself off the barstool and headed for the men's room. Frank placed a small stack of twenties under the salt shaker, grabbed his coat from the seat next to him, and slipped quietly out the door.

Chuck Delgado's filthy Cadillac was illegally parked by the dumpster while Ron's gleaming BMW sat in the first row. Frank kept to the shadows along the building and crossed to the Cadillac. As he'd hoped, Chuck had left it unlocked. Frank noiselessly opened the rear door and slid behind the driver's seat. He didn't have long to wait.

Chuck and Ron exited the restaurant together and headed for their cars. Chuck wedged himself behind the steering wheel, blew his nose loudly, and reached for the ignition.

"You should see a doctor about that," Haynes said quietly from the backseat. He smiled as Delgado lurched forward, startled.

Delgado met Frank's eyes in the rearview mirror. "You bastard!" he spat. "You scared the crap out of me. What is it about you, Frankie boy?" He turned as far in his seat as his girth would allow. "I thought you didn't want to be seen together."

"I don't, so turn around," Frank replied. "I have something pressing to discuss with you, Charles."

"Cut the crap, Frankie. What's up?"

"I've received reports that you made a threatening gesture toward Susan Martin when she was in the hospital."

"What're you doin' now, Frankie? Having me followed?"

"So you don't deny it?"

"If you mean do I deny doing this?" asked Delgado, pointing his finger at Frank in the rearview and lowering his thumb as if he were firing a gun. "Then no. I don't deny it." Delgado chortled. "And on her wedding day, to boot."

"What do you have against Susan Martin?" Frank asked. "She has nothing to do with any of this."

"She's related to that nosey bitch mayor," Delgado said. "That's even better. People seem to react much more quickly to threats against their loved ones than they do to threats against themselves."

"Don't stir up any more trouble," Frank said. "Your lawyers are sure you'll be acquitted. Use your head, for once."

"Easy for you to say when you weren't the one indicted. You're as dirty as I am, Frankie boy. Don't forget that. And if I want to make people pay for what's happened to me, that's my business, not yours. For all I know, that Martin bitch could be making other trouble for me. Best to take care of these situations early, before they get out of hand."

"You're wrong, Charles. This has to stop, and it has to stop now."

Delgado threw back his head and laughed. "Or what, Frankie boy? You gonna make me leave 'em alone?"

"I could if I needed to, Charles." Frank stared hard into Delgado's eyes.

"Then maybe you need to join my list, with Maggie and Susan Martin. I'm keepin' track of my enemies. Sounds like you've gone straight to the top, Frankie boy."

Frank Haynes' hand shook as he reached for the door handle.

Chapter 6

David Wheeler secured his seat belt as Grace Acosta slipped behind the wheel. "Thanks for giving us a ride home," he said, leaning between the seats to stroke Dodger behind the ears.

Grace started the engine. She glanced at David and smiled. "It's been really nice of you to come see my brother. It's made such a difference; you and Dodger are all he talks about."

David felt the color rise to his cheeks and turned toward the window. "No problem. Dodger loves doing this. We'll be here every day while he's in the hospital."

"Tommy's coming home tomorrow, so you won't need to come back on account of us."

David's heart sank to his shoes.

"That's why I'm driving today; my parents wanted to stay to make sure that they talk to the doctor." She stopped at the exit to the hospital parking lot. "You'll have to give me directions."

"Go right and then left at the second stop light."

Grace merged into traffic. "Thanks for showing me around school the other day. We've moved a lot, so I've changed schools before, but I was really nervous this time. It's been nice to know at least one other person."

"Why have you moved so often?"

"My dad gets offers to do research or be a visiting lecturer. He's very well thought of, and we've lived all over the world. I've seen tons of places and it's been fun, but I'm ready to put down roots and stay someplace for a while. My mom feels the same way, so my dad accepted a position at Highpointe College. He says we're going to plant a sapling in the yard and live here till it's forty feet tall." She sighed. "I hope so." She put on her blinker and moved into the left turn lane. "What does your father do?"

David cleared his throat. "My dad was mayor of Westbury, but he's dead now."

"Oh, gosh. I'm sorry." Grace brought her hand to his, where it rested on the console. "Here I am, whining about having to move when you've suffered a real tragedy. What happened? Was he sick?"

27

David was surprised that he was able to say the words without choking. "My dad was arrested for fraud and embezzlement—the same crimes Chuck Delgado is on trial for now. Are you familiar with the case?"

Grace shrugged. "I heard a little bit about it on the news, but I haven't paid much attention."

"My dad was supposed to have been part of it, but I feel sure he was framed. Anyway," David took a deep breath, "he committed suicide in jail."

Grace completed the left turn then pulled over to the curb of a residential street. "That's horrible, David. I'm so sorry. You're such a nice guy. You didn't deserve this."

David stared at his hands. "My dad didn't deserve what happened to him."

Grace sank back into her seat. "This must be terribly hard on your whole family. Do you have brothers and sisters?"

He shook his head. "It's just me and my mom. It's been awful. Mom got laid off shortly after he died. Everyone thought that she must have been in on it and that we had piles of money hidden somewhere. She didn't and we don't. She had a really hard time finding another job, and we lost our house to foreclosure—that's when Dr. Allen rented his house to us."

Grace squeezed his hand. The words tumbled out of David. "I got in trouble at school and almost got kicked out. They assigned an old guy to be my mentor, and he's helped me a lot. In fact, he's one of my best friends. Glenn Vaughn and Frank Haynes—he runs the no-kill animal shelter Forever Friends—helped me adopt Dodger and helped us get into pet therapy."

"Sounds like there are a lot of people on your side," Grace said, starting up the car and heading down David's street.

"That's the best thing about living in Westbury. People go out of their way to help each other. That's why I know my dad didn't cheat and embezzle. He grew up here and would never do that to the people of Westbury. I'm going to find a way to clear his name."

"How?"

"I'm not sure how I'll do it, but I have a good idea of where to start." David stared out the window, deep in thought. Dodger whined in the backseat, bringing David out of his reverie.

"Okay, boy. We're almost home." He turned to Grace. "It's that one there. On the right."

Grace pulled into the driveway.

David hopped out, opening the back door and retrieving Dodger. "Thanks for the ride."

"See you tomorrow," Grace said as she drove away.

—◦◦◦—

The next day after school, Grace saw David as she was walking down the hall with some of the girls from the theater group. She raised her hand and gestured for him to join them, but when he didn't see her wave she quickly brought her hand to her side.

"Is David a friend of yours?" one of the girls asked her.

Grace shrugged. "I met him at the hospital."

"Do you know the story about his family? You don't want to get near him," she continued as they reached the door to the theater department.

Grace frowned as she looked over her shoulder to see David hurry out the large glass door.

—◦◦◦—

David pretended that he didn't see Grace waving and continued on his way. He was headed for Chuck Delgado's liquor store on the other side of town. If he was lucky, he'd catch the three fifteen crosstown bus.

He rounded the corner of the gymnasium and was relieved to see the group of people waiting at the bus stop. He joined them just as the bus arrived.

Westbury High School was seven miles west of D's Liquor and Convenience Store. The bus made frequent stops, and it pulled to his destination almost thirty minutes later.

David crossed the street at the light and headed down the block to the nondescript two-story brick building with its garish neon sign. He paused at the edge of the parking lot and observed the store. The gas pumps were busy, and a steady stream of customers entered the store, many of them exiting with what he assumed were bottles of booze in brown paper sacks.

He rubbed his chin. In order to clear his father, he needed to find that missing spreadsheet. Maggie and Special Counsel Scanlon believed that Chuck Delgado had it in his possession. David needed to get close to him, and the only way he could think of to do that was to work for the man. Maybe then he'd get the chance to snoop around and find that spreadsheet or other incriminating evidence. He wasn't old enough to sell liquor and the gas pumps were all self-service. There must be something else he could do.

David made his way slowly around the perimeter of the parking lot to the back of the building, taking care not to draw anyone's attention. Two windows were set high into the brick, on the second floor. He wondered if Chuck Delgado's office was behind those windows. His pulse raced at the thought.

A delivery truck was parked near an open back door, and the driver was unloading cases of beer onto a hand cart. An old man stood to one side, shoulders hunched over a clipboard in his hand, making checkmarks on a sheet of paper.

"You're supposed to have someone here to help me unload, you know," the driver snarled at the old man as he hoisted another case of beer onto his cart.

"We don't have anybody right now," the old man replied without looking up from the clipboard.

"You haven't had anybody to help in months," the man said. "Tell that cheapskate boss of yours to hire someone."

"It's not that simple," the old man said. "Ever since his indictment, nobody wants to work for him."

"Tell him to up his pay," the driver said.

The old man shrugged.

The driver closed the rolling door on the back of his truck and secured the lock. "Show me where you want this."

The old man handed the driver the clipboard and motioned for the man to follow him.

"And next time, if you don't have someone to unload, I'm going to add a handling charge to that invoice," the driver said as he followed the old man into the building.

A smile spread slowly across David's face. He knew exactly what he needed to do.

Getting the job at D's Liquor and Convenience Store had been easy. The old man at the counter didn't bother to have David fill out an application or answer any questions. When David said he was looking for work and asked if they needed any help, the man looked him up and down, then jerked his thumb toward the back room.

"Stack those cases along the wall, break down that pile of empty boxes, and take the cardboard to the dumpster out back. When you're done with all that, come see me."

David tackled the tasks assigned to him. When he finished, he stepped through the vertical strips of plastic that separated the store from the back room. The old man spun around and jerked his glasses off his nose. "What? The work's not good enough for you?"

David stopped short. "No, sir. It's fine. I finished and you said to come see you when I was done."

The man stepped to the curtain and leaned into the back room. "Well ... so you have." He turned to David and studied his face. "You're William Wheeler's boy, aren't you?"

David nodded, feeling a lump rise in his throat.

"You look just like him." He replaced the glasses on his nose. "I'm sorry for your loss, son. I always liked your dad—he was a helluva nice guy."

David stood, rooted to the spot. The old man put a hand on David's shoulder.

"You're a heck of a good worker," he said to David. "We need somebody young and strong around here. You still in school?"

David nodded. "I can work every day after school—except Wednesdays—and I can come in on Sundays."

"Why not Wednesdays or Saturdays?"

"I take my therapy dog to the hospital or Fairview Terraces on Wednesdays, and I work at Forever Friends on Saturdays."

"You're a very busy kid," the man replied. "We can use you any time you can show up. We're always shorthanded." He pointed to a case of beer. "I'll show you how to stock shelves. If you can do that right, you'll be the best worker we've got around here."

David picked up the case of beer and followed the old man into the store. He was going to make sure he was the best worker they had. He'd find out if the upstairs room was Delgado's office, and he'd find a way for their "best worker" to get access to it.

Chapter 7

"He's here!" cried Sean Nash, letting the curtain drop back into place and running to the door of their apartment. He'd been watching the parking lot for the last thirty minutes. Frank Haynes was never late, and this time was no exception.

Loretta Nash put her hand on the door, holding it closed before Sean could fling it open. She looked at each of her three children in turn. Their faces shone with happiness and hope radiated from their eyes. She almost abandoned her planned admonishment, but took a deep breath and began. "We're going with Mr. Haynes to *look* at dogs today. We're not necessarily going to find one that we all like. That may take a while. Don't set your hearts on coming home with a dog today." She knew as she said this that her children would find a dog they couldn't live without at the shelter today. She'd have to be the bad guy and say no if the dog didn't fit their needs.

"We'll find a dog," Sean said.

"Mr. Haynes says the dog finds you," Marissa supplied, nodding her head knowingly.

Loretta was about to respond when she was interrupted by a firm knock on the door. Frank stood on the other side, dressed in jeans and a heavy jacket instead of his usual business suit and cashmere overcoat. He gave Loretta a quick kiss on the cheek and stepped across the threshold. "Ready to go get your dog?" he asked the three children gathered around him.

"Not you, too, Frank," Loretta said in exasperation. "I reminded them that we're just starting to look for a dog. We need to get the right one for us, and it may take time."

Frank realized his mistake. "Yes—exactly. Your mother is right, kids. We may not find your dog today, but we'll never know until we go look," he concluded and turned hopeful eyes to Loretta.

"Honestly, Frank, that's not much better." She smiled at him. She had to admit, his soft spot for animals was endearing. "Let's go." Her children yanked their coats off the coat rack and raced down the apartment stairs to Frank's waiting Mercedes sedan.

Loretta picked up her purse and locked the door behind her.

"I've looked through the dogs currently available for adoption at Forever Friends," he said, offering his arm as she joined him down the steps. "There are a number of good candidates."

"I'm still not convinced this is a good idea. I know you offered to keep the dog at your house until we can move out of this second-floor apartment, but God knows how long that will be. I'm not sure we should be doing this."

"Will it make your children profoundly happy?" He stopped and squeezed her elbow, turning to look at her. "And if it will, does anything else matter?"

Loretta rested the palms of her hands on his chest. "I guess so. I just don't know how I'm going to cope with one more thing."

"You're going to let me help you, that's how."

Loretta nodded her agreement as he opened her car door. She could hardly believe that this was the same man she had found cold and selfish when she first came to work for him little more than a year ago.

"So tell us about the dogs that you think are a good fit for us," she said as he started the car.

"They're all full grown, so you won't have to cope with chewing or handle potty training, and they're all small mixed breeds. Doxie plus terrier plus whatever. Cute as buttons, every one of them."

"If you say so. Remember, guys," Loretta said, facing the three grinning faces in the backseat, "the first squabble or harsh word, and we're outta there."

The three heads nodded in unison. "Don't worry, Mommy," Marissa said. "We'll be on our best behavior."

<hr/>

"It's an hour before the shelter opens to the public." Frank ushered Loretta and the kids into Forever Friends and locked the back door behind them. "We can look at the dogs and get acquainted with them without the hustle-and-bustle that occurs during normal hours." He gestured to a hallway on his right. "The dogs are down here. Follow me."

He led them past pens containing large mixed breeds, barking loudly. Nicole covered her ears, but Sean stopped in front of a pen holding a medium-sized black-and-gray dog that sat quietly wagging her tail and drooling. He stuck his fingers through the grate, and the dog instantly swiped them with her tongue. Sean looked at the tag on the front of the pen. "This one's a cattle dog and Australian shepherd mix," he called after his family. "It says she's two years old and she's shy." He turned to the dog. "Hello, girl," he cooed, attempting to scratch between her ears.

"What about this one?" he called.

"She's too big for us, Sean," Loretta replied. "That sort of dog needs room to run, and we don't have it."

Sean turned to Frank. "Does your house have room for her to run, Mr. Haynes?"

Frank nodded in the affirmative.

"Even if Mr. Haynes keeps the dog for us at first, we need one that we can provide a good home for in the long run. I'm sorry, Sean. That dog is just too big, honey," Loretta said, closing the discussion.

Sean gave one last look at the dog before he turned away.

"This one is sweet," Marissa said, pointing to a shaggy white dog with short ears and dark eyes and nose.

"That's the one I like, too," Nicole said.

Loretta read his tag. "This says he's one-and-a-half years old and a mix of terrier and schnauzer." She looked at Frank. "What do you think? Is that a good mix? Will this boy have a good temperament?"

"He looks like an excellent dog," Frank said, kneeling down to examine the animal. "Let's take him out for a visit in the 'get acquainted area.' It's the only way to really tell for sure."

"I didn't know you could do that," Loretta replied as Frank took a key from his pocket and unlocked the pen. He scooped the dog under his arm and proceeded down the hall, the three children trailing close behind.

Loretta followed, enjoying the sight of her children and Frank having fun together. Was she a fool for falling for this guy? The man was her boss for heaven's sake; another good reason to stop this before it went any further. Even as she thought this, she knew she was too late. She'd fallen for Frank Haynes hook, line, and sinker. If she got her heart broken, again, she'd just have to deal with it.

Loretta stepped into the get acquainted area as Frank directed her children to sit on the low benches along the perimeter. "He's scared right now," Frank said. "Remember—there's five of us and only one of him. He needs to sniff around to get his bearings."

"Here, boy," Sean called, waving and snapping his fingers at the excited dog.

Frank held his hand out to Sean. "Don't call him. That's only confusing him. Let him come to you."

Sean sat back in a huff.

"He'll come to you, Sean," Frank said. "Don't worry. The key to animals is that they have to trust you. You're the master and you need to be in charge—animals want that—but you have to be sensitive to what they need, too."

Loretta watched as the dog approached her oldest daughter tentatively.

"Hold out your hand to him, Marissa. Slowly. No sudden movements. And don't try to grab him or pick him up," Frank said.

Marissa did as Frank directed and the animal sniffed her hand.

"Can I pat his head?" Marissa asked softly.

"Sure," Frank replied.

Marissa gently scratched between his ears. The dog wagged his tail wildly and sprang into her lap. Marissa buried her face in the dog's fur as Nicole slid next to her sister on the bench. The dog squirmed until he was distributed on both laps, enjoying hugs and kisses from both girls.

"This is the one we want," Marissa and Nicole said in unison.

Loretta approached her daughters and knelt in front of them. The dog hopped out of their laps and went to Loretta. "What do you think, Sean?"

"Can he play fetch or catch a Frisbee?" Sean looked over his shoulder at Frank.

"If he can't, you could teach him."

Sean nodded. "I was sort of thinking I'd like to have a therapy dog, like Dodger. Go to hospitals and stuff."

"You could see about training him. He might be a bit hyper," Frank replied and caught Loretta's eye. "Is that why you liked the dog down the hall that you saw earlier? Does she remind you of Dodger?"

Sean shrugged. "Maybe. But I'm okay with this guy," he said, tousling the dog's ears. "My sisters like him and he's small, so Mom will let us keep him." He looked quickly at Loretta. "You will let us get him, won't you?"

The dog jumped into Loretta's lap and licked her face. She sputtered and wiped the slobber off with the back of her hand. "Yes. If Frank is still willing to keep him for us for a while, I'm fine with him."

The girls leapt to their feet and rushed to Frank. "Thank you, Mr. Haynes," Marissa said as Nicole hugged him. "This is the best day ever."

"Do we need to come back when they're open to fill out the paperwork and pick him up?" Loretta asked.

Frank shook his head. "I'll take care of that for you. Let's get him out of here before they open. I think we should stop at the pet store on the way to my place. You'll need to pick out a collar and leash and we probably should buy some toys. What do you think?"

The girls cheered. Frank fastened a free loaner leash bearing the Forever Friends logo around the dog's neck and handed the leash to Sean. "Can you handle him for us?"

Sean smiled and nodded.

"You'll need to come up with a name for him, too," Frank said as they piled into his car. The dog settled onto Sean's lap.

"What about Snowball?" Marissa suggested. "He looks like a snowball."

Nicole nodded vigorously.

Loretta laughed. "That's a fitting name, all right. Sean—what do you think?"

"That's okay," he said quietly.

"Snowball it is, then." Loretta said. "We'll get a name tag for him today."

Frank pulled up to the door of the pet store ten minutes later. "Why don't you start shopping? I'll park the car and be right in." He turned to Sean. "We don't know if he's trained on the leash so carry him and put him in a cart."

Loretta patted Frank's hand and mouthed *thank you.*

Frank watched as the electric door closed behind the four people who had become so dear to him. He didn't notice the black sedan with darkly tinted windows that pulled into the lot behind him. Frank slipped the car into a parking space, pulled out his cell phone, and dialed Forever Friends. "Is David Wheeler there yet?" he asked the receptionist. "I need to speak to him."

Frank paused while David came to the phone. "Do you know that cattle dog–Aussie mix that came in last week? Nice, calm girl?" He listened to David's response. "That's the one. I'd like to adopt her for Sean Nash. Would you go pull her papers and put them on my desk, so no one else adopts her? And when you get a chance, can you spend some time with her? See if you think she'd make a good therapy dog. Sean's pretty young to be a handler, but he's interested in doing what you and Dodger do. I'll help him, if I can."

Chapter 8

Maggie looked up from her computer screen when she heard the knock on her office door. She checked her watch. It was already noon. "Come in," she called.

Councilmember Tonya Holmes entered the room. Tonya didn't walk into a room, Maggie had decided years ago, she entered. At six feet tall and always immaculately dressed in a tailored suit and pearls, Tonya made an entrance.

"Turn that thing off and get your coat. We're going to lunch, and we won't be back in an hour."

Maggie laughed and reached for her purse. "You're bossy today, aren't you?"

"When am I ever *not* bossy?"

"Good point." Maggie smiled at her ally in town government and one of her dearest friends in Westbury. "What's up?"

"I want to hear how Susan's doing, and I have something I'd like to talk to you about."

Maggie looked at the paperwork on her desk and raised an eyebrow.

"It can wait. I called Pete's Bistro, and they're holding a table for us. We'd better go. It's cold, but it's not wet or windy. Why don't we walk?"

"I'd love to. Going back and forth to my car is the only exercise I'm getting these days," Maggie said, pointing to her waistline. "And it shows."

⁂

"I should've ordered a salad, but I can smell the barbeque sauce from here," Tonya said, as the server left their table. "So—how is Susan doing? Those superbugs are horrific—she could have died. It seems so unfair. Donating a kidney to a half-sister you've only just learned about and then contracting an infection that almost kills you?"

Maggie nodded and ran her hands over her eyes. "It's hard for me to think about. But she's getting stronger every day."

"She was released from the hospital last week, wasn't she?"

"Yes. She's recuperating at Rosemont. Aaron had to go back to California to resume his orthopedic surgical residency, and she's staying with us for a while."

"What a shame that they have to be apart right at the start of their marriage. It was a lovely wedding, Maggie." She grabbed one of the lemons the server had just dropped off and squeezed it into her iced tea. "Very meaningful. I'll never forget it—and not because it was held in the hospital chapel. The feeling of love and gratitude in that room was palpable."

"It was nice, wasn't it?" Maggie sighed.

"So what's she doing all day?"

"Susan volunteered to help Alex write motions for the case against Delgado. She's been working up a storm, actually. Those two get along famously. I think they're both secretly wishing they could go on forever. But she'll be well enough to go home soon, and her medical leave from her law firm will run out, so she'll go back to work."

"And to her new husband."

"Of course. I think she's staying busy so that she doesn't miss him as much."

"Aaron's a very sweet guy."

"He sure is. He's even coming back out here so that he can fly with her when she goes home. He doesn't want her to have to travel alone."

The server brought their lunches, and they tucked into their pulled-pork sandwiches, the day's special.

"This is phenomenal," Maggie said. She cut her sandwich in half. "I'm going to bring this home to John. Pete has a way with barbecue, doesn't he?"

"What doesn't he have a way with?" Tonya asked.

"So what is this 'other thing' you wanted to talk to me about?"

"I know how busy you are, Maggie, and I almost refused to ask you this. But I think you'd be terrific at it, and more importantly, I think you'd really enjoy it."

Maggie groaned. "If I take on one more thing, John is going to shoot me. And I'll gladly hand him the gun."

"Fair enough, but hear me out." Tonya laid her fork on the table and leaned forward. "We've got new neighbors—the Acostas—next door.

They're super-nice people. We had them over for dinner last Sunday night. He's a professor at Highpointe and putting together a panel on jobs in the new economy and is looking for speakers, specifically, a forensic account- ant, and I told him the best forensic accountant is right here in Westbury." She touched Maggie's hand. "You."

Maggie snorted. "Thank you for the compliment, but I'm hardly the best."

"There are a lot of people in this town who think you are," she said, raising her glass to Maggie and taking a long sip. "Anyway, Professor Acosta didn't feel comfortable contacting you since he's never met you, so I offered to ask you. It's a day-long career event, but you'd only have to show up to the panel discussion itself. And there'd be a few conference calls to plan the panel—but that's it. They're scheduling it for a late afternoon in February."

Maggie picked up her water glass and took a drink.

"Admit it—you'd be fabulous. This is in your wheelhouse."

Maggie nodded and a slow smile slid across her lips. "It's tempting. I'd enjoy it, that's for sure. I just don't think I have time for fun extracurricu- lars these days. Not with the trouble this town is in."

"You can take an afternoon to do something you'll enjoy. All the prob- lems will still be there when you get back. It's not like you'd be out on some boondoggle. You'd be helping the local college. If you'd like to do this, say yes."

Maggie glanced out the window toward Town Hall. When she turned back to Tonya, she was smiling. "Yes," she said. "Tell that neighbor of yours I'd be happy to participate."

Chapter 9

Loretta Nash swung her car around a black sedan with darkly tinted windows parked on the roadside and pulled through the open gate and onto the circular drive that swept in front of Frank Haynes' home. She'd driven by his house before, but the tall hedge row running parallel to the road and the mature trees obscured a view of anything except the roofline. She slowed, scanning the facade of the stately stone home. *Frank certainly has done well for himself,* she thought. With its mullioned windows and multiple chimneys, it looked like a smaller version of Rosemont.

She pulled to a stop by the front walkway, and her kids leapt out of the car.

Sean bounded up the steps ahead of his sisters. "Where's Snowball?" he asked, brushing past Frank who was standing at the front door.

"He's out back, with the others," he called after him.

Sean stopped and turned to face Frank.

"Go ahead. Through there." Frank smiled, pointing to a hallway that lead to the left.

Sean took off at a run while Loretta and his sisters came through the front door.

"Your dogs are outside," Frank said to the girls. "Go join your brother." He gestured in the direction Sean had just gone.

"Dogs?" Loretta asked.

"That's what I wanted to talk to you about," Frank said.

She arched an eyebrow.

"I think you should get Sean the cattle dog–Aussie mix that he took such a shine to at the shelter."

Loretta's shoulders dropped. "Frank! Why did you do that? I can't take on a dog that size."

"Hear me out, Loretta. I saw firsthand how a dog like that turned David Wheeler's life around. Hell—a dog like that turned my life around when I was a kid." He put both of his hands on her arms and turned her gently to him. "You saw Sean's face yesterday when he was with this dog. They need each other. I'm prepared to keep her here permanently, if necessary. She and my dog, Sally, are getting along just fine. In fact, a younger more active dog will be good for that old border collie."

Loretta sighed and reached up to kiss him. "You've got an incredibly kind heart, Frank Haynes. If you're not careful, everyone in town is going to learn what a softy you are."

"Good grief, no. That would be terrible for business. Can you keep my secret?"

"I'll do my best, but I don't know how long you'll be able to hide your shiny armor and that white steed you've been riding around on."

Frank blushed and pulled her close. She was tilting her mouth to his when they heard footsteps racing down the hallway, accompanied by the unmistakable sound of paws clipping along on the tile. They pulled apart just as Sean burst into the room, the cattle dog mix at his heels.

"Mr. Haynes!" he cried, almost out of breath. "You got her!"

Frank nodded.

Sean threw his arms around him, forcing Frank to step back to keep his balance. "Thank you. I hated leaving her there. I kept waking up all night long, seeing her face behind the bars of the cage." Sean sniffed and wiped his sleeve across his eyes. "I'm so happy she's here."

Frank glanced at Loretta over the top of Sean's head. She was pressing her fingers into the circles below her eyes and blinking rapidly.

"What're you going to call her?" Frank asked, bending down to stroke the dog prancing at his feet.

"Is she mine?" Sean asked, unable to keep the yearning out of his voice.

Frank raised his eyebrows at Loretta.

Loretta nodded. "She's yours, honey. I'm not sure how soon we'll be able to bring her home with us, but if Frank will keep her for us, you can have her."

Sean dropped to his knees and threw his arms around the squirming animal. "I decided last night what I'd call you: Daisy."

"Daisy will need to be trained, and she'll need lots of exercise," Frank said. "She's your dog, so you'll have to do these things. Are you ready to take on this responsibility?"

Sean stood and nodded solemnly.

"I thought so," Frank said. "We'll get a list of obedience classes from Dr. Allen. We'll find something you can do after school."

"Let's go check on your sisters and Snowball," Loretta said, heading down the hallway.

"I took both dogs out on a leash this morning," Frank said. "They've each had some training. Why don't we all go to the park for a walk?"

"It's supposed to start snowing this afternoon, so the sooner the better," Loretta said. She opened the back door to find the girls and the dogs running in a circle. At this point, it was impossible to tell who was chasing whom.

"We're going to the park," Loretta called to her daughters, cupping her hands around her mouth.

Marissa turned to her mother and Snowball bounded up to Loretta, placing muddy paws on her clean jeans. Loretta bent and accepted a face-washing of doggie kisses. "I'd better get used to this, with all of you dog lovers in my life," she said over her shoulder to Frank.

"Can we put the sweater we bought yesterday on Snowball?" Marissa asked her mother.

"He's got a fur coat; he doesn't really need it—" Frank began but stopped himself when he caught Marissa's expression, "but he'll probably look very stylish in it, so of course you should."

Marissa beamed. "It's red plaid and matches his collar and leash."

Frank nodded thoughtfully. "I remember. Excellent choices. I should get a sweater for Sally. Maybe you and Nicole can help me pick one out?"

Marissa nodded vigorously.

Loretta stood. "Okay, everybody. Let's get going."

Frank Haynes struggled to keep the undisciplined Sally at heel while Sean and Daisy walked a short distance ahead. Nicole skipped along next to Marissa and Snowball, who pranced politely on his leash. Visitors to the park smiled at the two girls and their dog decked out in his jaunty attire.

Loretta slipped her hand through Frank's arm and watched her children and their dogs. "Maybe you and Sally should attend that obedience school with Sean," she teased.

Frank cut his gaze to her. "Might not be a bad idea. I've tried to train her, but I swear—Sally is the most stubborn dog I've ever owned."

"She's awfully sweet, though." Loretta defended her.

Up ahead, Nicole began waving her arms over her head and took off running.

"Where are you going?" Loretta called, dropping Frank's arm and starting after her.

Nicole stopped and pointed. "Tommy."

"Tommy's the little boy that we met at the hospital when Nicole was in for her last checkup. The one that had eye surgery?" Loretta said over her shoulder to Frank. She squinted in the direction Nicole was pointing. "It looks like he and his older sister are walking their dog today, too."

"Can I go say hi?" Nicole looked up at her mother, then at Frank.

Loretta nodded.

Nicole raced to her new friend. Marissa and Snowball followed, with Frank and Loretta bringing up the rear.

"Hi, Tommy," Nicole called. "Is this your dog?" she asked, pointing to the corgi at Tommy's heels.

Tommy nodded. "Did you get a dog?" he asked as Marissa joined them.

"Yesterday." Nicole clapped her hands. "He's called Snowball."

The two dogs began the intimate sniffing that dogs are so fond of. Grace squatted down to pet the Nash's new dog. "What a cutie," she remarked. "And such a beautiful sweater."

Marissa beamed. "We got everything to match," she said, pointing to the collar and leash.

"I'm Nicole's mom," Loretta said to Grace. "Nicole told me all about you two. How's your brother doing?"

"He's doing great. He only has to wear the patch outside, in direct sunlight. His eye is still very sensitive. They expect that to clear up in a few days."

"That's great news." Loretta looked at the girl. "How are you doing? Are you happy in your new school?"

Grace shrugged. "I think it'll be fine. I was happy to move here. And I've met a couple of people."

"Any cute boys?"

"Well ... I've met one really nice boy, but I'm not sure that he's interested in me." Grace sighed.

"Is he in your class at school?"

"He is, but I actually got to know him at the hospital after Tommy's surgery. He visited us with his therapy dog."

"David Wheeler—of course! He's a very nice boy. He and Dodger visited Nicole when she was so ill. They're part of the reason we added two dogs to the family." Loretta looked to the other side of the park for Sean and Daisy.

"Speak of the devil," Frank said. "David and Dodger are over there with Sean and Daisy." He raised his hand over his head and gestured to the boys to join them.

Grace tucked her hair behind her ears and pulled at her scarf.

"You look lovely," Loretta whispered, leaning toward her.

David Wheeler and Dodger followed behind as Daisy led Sean to them.

"Dodger!" Tommy cried, kneeling to greet the dog.

"Hey, everybody," David said. He nodded to Grace.

Frank extended his hand to shake David's. "Giving him some exercise before you head to the hospital?" Frank asked.

David shook his head. "I've got a new job, so we're only doing therapy visits one afternoon a week."

Frank inhaled sharply. "Do you need more hours? I can increase your schedule at Forever Friends. Or do you need a raise?"

"No. Nothing like that. I love my job at Forever Friends."

"Where are you working?" Frank asked.

"D's Liquor and Convenience Store."

Frank's head snapped back. "Delgado's liquor store? On the other side of town?"

David nodded.

"Why in the world are you working there?"

"I just wanted to get some different experience."

"What's he got you doing?"

"Unloading trucks and stocking shelves. Manual labor."

"Doesn't sound like valuable experience to me. What's he paying you? Is that it?"

"Minimum wage. It's not about the money." David cut his eyes to Grace.

"Then I don't understand …" Frank began as Loretta put her hand on his arm.

"You remember Grace?" she interjected, drawing the girl forward.

"Hey. How are you?" David asked.

"Fine. I saw you after school last week, but I don't think you saw me."

"I did, but I was in a hurry to catch the bus to get to my new job."

Grace drew a deep breath and continued. "Tommy and I are going to get a pizza when we're done here. Want to come with us?"

"I'd like to, but I have to be at work in an hour." David sighed heavily and shifted his weight from foot to foot. "I'd better get going."

"Stay away from Chuck Delgado," Frank said sternly. "He's not someone I want you getting involved with."

"Don't worry, Frank," David replied, not telling him that getting involved with Chuck Delgado was exactly why he'd taken the job. He glanced shyly at Grace. "See you around."

Grace smiled at him and his heart turned over.

———

"The kids all had fun today, didn't they?" Loretta asked Frank later that night as they cuddled on her sofa after her children had gone to bed.

"Me, too," Frank chimed in.

"Tommy and Grace seem nice. It's good to see my kids making friends here. Westbury is starting to feel like home to all of us. I've never felt like I was part of a community before."

Frank kissed her on the nose. "Glad to hear it."

She shifted, so she could look into his eyes. "Did you see the way Grace and David looked at each other? I saw sparks fly."

"You might be right about that."

"I just hope he has time for a girlfriend. He needs to have some fun. You're only a teenager once." She sighed. "He's such a hard worker, what with Forever Friends and helping Sam Torres with his handyman work, plus his pet therapy visits. And now this new job of his—working for Chuck Delgado of all people." Loretta shivered. "You know how I loathe that perverted creep."

Frank's expression turned to steel. "I agree with you about Delgado. I was going to warn you about him. He's more dangerous than ever." He tilted her chin so that he could look directly into her eyes. "I don't want you anywhere near him. If you see him—even just his car, in the distance—you are to get as far away as possible."

Loretta drew back. "I know, Frank. I won't get close to the guy." She searched his face. "Has something new happened to alarm you? What's Delgado done now?"

"Let's just say I know what I'm talking about. Promise me, Loretta," he said, and the tone of his voice sent shivers down her spine.

"I promise. The kids and I will steer clear of him." She traced his cheek with her finger. "And I want you to stay away from him, too, Frank."

Frank took her hands in his and kissed her open palms before looking away.

———

The man rolled down a darkly tinted window and flicked the ash from his cigarette onto the asphalt. He punched Chuck Delgado's number into his cell phone and drew on the cigarette.

Delgado picked up on the seventh ring. "Yeah?" he barked into the phone.

"He spent the day with that good-lookin' assistant of his and her kids. Went to the park with them."

Delgado snorted. "Bastard leads a boring life. Anything else?"

"They met up with David Wheeler and that one-eyed dog of his at the park. And some other kids."

"Frankie's close to William Wheeler's kid. I think he feels guilty that the boy's old man killed himself in jail." Delgado chuckled. "Best thing that could have happened—for both Frankie and me. Keep watching—I need to know what he's up to."

Chapter 10

Maggie pulled into a parking spot at Highpointe College reserved for visiting dignitaries. The administration building, where the panel was to be held later in the afternoon, was directly in front of her. She'd arrived early, so she could explore the campus on her own.

She turned her coat collar up around her ears and followed a path that skirted the imposing building and lead into an open area labeled "Common" on the college map. The common was flanked by ornate brick buildings dating from the late 1800s. Sidewalks created a labyrinth of pathways.

Maggie paused, taking in the sights and sounds of a college campus. There was something so solid and timeless about the scene before her. The common was scattered with men and women, alone and in groups, some walking purposefully and others meandering as if they had all the time in the world. Although their style of dress would have been different, Maggie knew that the scene before her would have played out a century or more ago in much the same way.

She inhaled deeply and began to walk. She had enough time to circle the perimeter of the common before the panel discussion. She'd spent two decades of her life intimately involved with Windsor College during Paul's tenure there—first when he was a professor, then a dean, and finally as the college president. If he hadn't died of a sudden heart attack, she might still be there.

Maggie picked her way across the frozen grass to a bench nestled next to a large pine tree. She brushed aside a smattering of needles and sat gingerly on the edge of the seat. Who was she kidding? If Paul hadn't died, how long could he have kept his embezzlement from the college a secret? Their marriage had definitely soured by then. Would he have left her for Loretta Nash? She shook her head, as if she could banish these unanswered—and unanswerable—questions. None of it mattered, anyway. She was here now, married to the love of her life, living in her dream home, and doing her best in a job that challenged and frustrated her in equal measure.

She leaned back, breathing in the crisp air. Paul or no Paul—she loved a college campus. She'd been happy at Windsor, and she was relieved to find that Paul's memory didn't spoil this experience for her now. She checked her watch and turned her attention back to Highpointe. It was time to find Professor Acosta.

———

Maggie surveyed the sea of faces before her in the packed auditorium. Most of them were in their early to mid-twenties, she surmised, with their whole lives before them. Eager and hopeful. They'd been an attentive audience. She'd forgotten how much she enjoyed being around young people. She smiled at the group as Professor Acosta made his closing remarks.

When he'd finished, she picked up her purse from the floor and turned to the gentleman on the panel seated next to her. He was an expert on supply-chain management and had given a lengthy and rather dry dissertation on the subject. She smiled politely and congratulated him on his presentation before turning to exit.

"Mayor Martin!" a young man called from the audience. "A few of us were wondering if you'd like to join us for a cup of coffee—if you have time," he added quickly. "We know how busy you are."

Maggie looked at the small group of students he was pointing to. "I'd love to," she stammered. "Let me see if I have any messages." She pulled her phone out of her purse and scrolled through the texts from her assistant and from Alex.

"I'm afraid I'm needed back at Town Hall," she said. "But I can spare a few minutes to answer any questions now," she said, looking to Professor Acosta, who nodded his approval.

The young man gestured to the other students to join them. Maggie fielded a few specific questions about her academic specialty, forensic accounting, but soon found herself dispensing hopeful common sense advice like a wise grandmother. She was in her element and forgot about the urgent matter awaiting her attention at Town Hall. None of the students made a move to leave, and they would have gone on into the evening if Professor Acosta hadn't gently intruded to tell them that it was after hours and the maintenance crew needed to lock the building.

Maggie turned to the group. "I've enjoyed meeting all of you and wish you the best of success in your college careers and afterwards."

"Maybe you can come speak to us again?" a woman asked.

"That's just what I was thinking," Professor Acosta said, smiling at Maggie. "Let me talk to our president and coordinate with Mayor Martin. I'm sure we can entice her to come back," he told the students. He offered Maggie his arm and escorted her to the rear entrance.

"You were quite the hit," he said as he walked with her through the common toward the parking lot.

"That was a great panel you put together," she replied. "Such a good idea. These kids are hungry for words of hope about their futures."

"You were the only one talking about that." Professor Acosta turned to face her. "You feel a real connection with these kids, don't you?"

Maggie nodded. "I guess I do. My late husband was a college president, and I've spent the majority of my adult life in this atmosphere," she said, her arm drawing a semi-circle in front of her. "I had no idea, until today, how much I loved it."

Professor Acosta smiled. "You're an academic at heart. Maybe you should come back here."

"I don't have a Ph.D., and I'm not planning to get one. I'm afraid college life isn't in the cards for me."

Professor Acosta shrugged and opened her car door for her. "You just never know what life has in store."

If you only knew how true that's been in my life, Maggie thought as she pulled out of the parking lot.

———

Susan turned over in bed and brushed her unruly blond hair off her face and propped herself on her elbow to look at her husband's sleeping face. He stirred and cracked one eye. He reached for her and pulled her to him. "Can't sleep? Everything all right?" he asked, suddenly awake and concerned.

She snuggled into his shoulder. "I'm fine. Now that you're with me, everything's perfect. Thank you for coming back here to travel with me."

"I wouldn't have it any other way," he said. "Excited to finally go home?"

Susan sighed. "Excited to be back with you. Not so excited to return to my practice at the firm."

Aaron shifted his weight, so he could look at her. "Has something happened?"

"Not with the firm," Susan said. "With me. I love working with your brother. I've never felt so comfortable, so collegial with another lawyer. Our thought processes work the same way. Even the most complicated issues are easy to dissect and tackle together."

"Does Alex feel the same way?"

She nodded against his shoulder.

"And you like Westbury? What about the winter climate? I like snow, but I'm not sure my California girl, here, is in favor of it."

"You've got me there." Susan yawned. "It doesn't matter anyway. We go back day after tomorrow."

"We'd better get some sleep. Knowing your mother, she'll have the entire town here tomorrow to say goodbye to you."

John Allen woke at four fifteen, his internal clock long adapted to early morning veterinary surgeries, and crept noiselessly to the bathroom so as not to wake his sleeping wife. He was halfway across the room when he saw the sliver of light under the door from the chandelier over the stairway. He shook his head. His wife was up and at it, undoubtedly tending to some detail related to Susan's imminent departure.

Maggie was, indeed, busy downstairs. She'd thrown on her robe and slippers thirty minutes earlier, unable to quiet her mind. She'd been making lists and going over her timetables for the impromptu open house she was hosting that afternoon for anyone who wanted to drop in and see Susan and Aaron before they left the following morning.

She'd ordered trays of finger foods from Pete's: chicken skewers in spicy chili sauce, street tacos, crudités and hummus, baked brie with figs and walnuts, and a slew of desserts. John had stocked up on wine and sodas over the weekend. All she needed to do now was put a cloth on the dining room table and set out her serving pieces.

John came downstairs fifteen minutes later to find Maggie wrestling her heaviest damask tablecloth over her ironing board. Bubbles was at her feet, batting a tentative paw at the fabric. "No one will ever notice if that thing isn't ironed," he remarked.

Maggie held up a hand to silence him. "Maybe so, but I can hear my grandmother's voice in my ear: 'If you're going to invite people into your home, make the extra effort to show them you care. Details matter.'" She blew a strand of hair off her damp forehead and bent down to shoo Bubbles away. "I realize this is insane, but I'm powerless over my past. At least as far as ironing tablecloths goes."

John leaned in and kissed the top of her head. "You can't fool me, Mrs. Allen. You're a traditionalist, and I think you enjoy all this." He gestured to the ironing board.

She smiled at him and shrugged.

"What time do you need me home?"

"We're starting at four. I'll pick up the food, and Susan and Aaron will help me set it out, so you don't need to cut your day short. Just get here when you can."

"I've got a light schedule today, so I'll be able to lend a hand." He took her chin in his hand. "It'll all be fine. These are our closest friends. Don't overdo."

Aaron carried the last tray of food into the kitchen and set it on the counter. Maggie was busy rearranging items in her refrigerator to make room for everything. "Would you take these into the laundry room and put them on top of the washer?" Maggie asked, handing him bottles of ketchup and mustard and jars of pickles. "I need the room, and these can sit out for a while."

"How many did you say were coming?"

Maggie shut the refrigerator door and slumped against it. "Everybody who was at your wedding. Plus a few more."

"Did your daughter inherit your penchant for entertaining?"

"I'm afraid she did." Maggie patted his arm as she picked up two jars of olives and lead the way to the laundry room. "Speaking of my daughter, is she taking a nap?"

Aaron nodded. "I insisted on it. John warned me last night that this probably wouldn't be a small gathering."

"She doesn't have to get herself all gussied up," Maggie said. "Why don't we let her sleep until three thirty?"

Susan was on her way down the stairs at three forty-five as Maggie was going up, her hands on the collars of the dogs. "Eve and Roman will just get in the way. I'm confining them to our room."

"Good plan. What about Bubbles, Blossom, and Buttercup?"

"Cats are smart enough to hide during a party. We won't catch a glimpse of them."

Maggie continued up the stairs when the doorbell rang. "Would you get that, sweetheart?"

"Smart money says it'll be either Judy Young or Joan Torres, coming early to help," Susan called after her mother. She opened the door and was gratified to see that not one but both of the women greeted her warmly.

"Sorry we didn't get here earlier," Judy said, stepping past Susan. "I couldn't get one of my vendors off the phone. The shop usually isn't busy in the late afternoon, so I didn't think I'd have any trouble getting away."

Joan Torres hugged Susan. "You look well, my dear. I'm so glad."

"Come on in. I was upstairs napping, so I don't know if Mom needs any help or not."

The three women entered the dining room where everything was beautifully arrayed on gleaming silver platters.

"Oh! She's used the vintage silver that she found in the attic," Judy said, clearly delighted.

"Yep," Susan replied. "Mom said that if we were going to keep it, we were going to use it. No point in leaving it hidden away in tarnish-proof bags."

Judy nodded approvingly. "Quite right."

Aaron came up behind Susan and encircled her with his arms.

Joan smiled at them. "Maybe you should consider moving here. Just think—" she began before she was interrupted by the doorbell. "We'll have to continue this later. I'll go stand by the door. People don't arrive late to a Rosemont party."

"Has Maggie started the coffee yet?" Judy asked.

Aaron shrugged.

"I'll see to things in the kitchen. This is your night. It's almost another wedding reception. Go enjoy yourselves."

———

Every person invited showed up to wish the young couple—who'd come so close to losing each other—a long and happy life together. Fires crackled in the great fireplaces in the living room and the library. Marc Benson played show tunes on the piano in the conservatory.

Alex leaned against the wall, beaming with pride at his accomplished partner. It was nice to be back at Rosemont as a guest. He remembered the weeks that he and Marc had stayed there—under Maggie's watchful eye—while he struggled to recover his strength and mobility after their devastating car accident. Much like Susan had just done after surviving a serious staph infection, he realized. Rosemont was a healing place—there was no denying it.

———

The party was winding down when the last guests arrived. John opened the door to find Loretta Nash and her three children standing on the threshold.

"Come in," he said, motioning them inside.

"Nicole wanted to say goodbye to her sister," Loretta said quickly. "Sean and Marissa wanted to come, too. I hope this is okay."

"Of course it is," John replied. "They're all in the conservatory. There's plenty of food, so be sure to help yourselves."

Loretta shook her head. "I'll wait outside. I don't want to intrude."

"Don't be silly."

"Frank Haynes drove us here, so I'll just sit with him."

"Nonsense," John replied. "Frank should join the party, too."

Loretta hesitated.

"I insist," John said. "Go on in with your kids, and I'll get Frank." He pointed them toward the conservatory and slipped out the front door to Frank's Mercedes idling in the driveway. Frank rolled down his window as John approached.

"Shut that thing off and get in here, Frank." The two men looked at each other. "You're welcome in our home. You—of all people—have a right to be here. We've never thanked you for allowing us to buy out your interest in Rosemont. I guess we didn't know what to say. Maggie's written and discarded a dozen letters."

Frank shook his head. "Not necessary. It was a business decision." He glanced at John and knew that John didn't believe him.

"It's cold out here," John said. "Come on."

Frank shut off the ignition and followed John up the stone steps to the massive mahogany door. He was surprised that he didn't feel any of the familiar emotions he'd felt before when stepping through the front door of the home he'd coveted his entire life. No regret. No envy.

"Food's in the dining room," John said, pointing to the large table of food. "And everybody's in the conservatory."

Frank nodded and made his way into the dining room. He picked up a plate, but he wasn't hungry. He walked to the conservatory door and observed the scene unfolding before him. Susan was sitting on a large ottoman, Nicole in her lap. Marissa was showing Susan her new shoes, and Sean was sitting on the piano bench with Marc. Loretta and Maggie were standing companionably together. This must be what having a warm, loving family and a lot of good friends was like. No wonder people described it as priceless.

His reverie was interrupted when Alex entered the room from the kitchen. The two men eyed each other silently. Frank was the first to speak.

"I hear you're working very hard on the case against Delgado."

"Of course I am," Alex snapped.

Frank stepped around the table and spoke to Alex in a low voice. "I want you to get Delgado, Alex. You need to get Delgado."

Chapter 11

Forest Smith turned his car out of the parking lot of First Methodist Church. His massive workload as second-chair attorney in the case against Chuck Delgado had kept him at the office late. He hadn't had time for dinner before the session with his addiction recovery support group. The meeting was now over, and he headed toward McDonald's on his way home. He'd hate himself in the morning for breaking his strict diet, but a Big Mac sounded delicious right now.

The streets of Westbury were nearly deserted after nine o'clock, and the sky was thick with clouds that obliterated the sliver of a moon. Forest noted the headlights in his rearview mirror shortly after he exited the parking lot.

Another car would not normally be cause for alarm, but these weren't normal times. Forest shook his head. When he had told Alex he was being blackmailed by Delgado, they'd decided to play along. Chuck believed Forest had been secretly working for him and had removed key evidence from the state's case. But if that creep ever discovered the truth, Forest would be a dead man.

The car was still following him. Forest drove past the entrance to McDonald's and continued for another quarter mile, then made a quick U-turn. He passed the car and recognized Delgado's corpulent frame behind the wheel. The two men locked eyes for a brief moment. Delgado was alone in his car.

Forest put on his blinker and pulled into an alley behind an auto body shop. He put his car in park but didn't cut the ignition. He paused, wondering if he should text Alex or the police chief to let them know what was happening. Delgado swung into the alley and pulled the nose of his car up to Forest's bumper. He lumbered out of his car, making his way to the passenger side door. Forest unlocked it, and Delgado wedged himself into the seat next to him.

"You need to get yourself a decent-sized car, buddy boy. This thing is a tin can."

"Did you follow me tonight to give me automotive advice?"

"Don't be a smartass. I own you, remember?"

"I think you're forgetting something. When I gave you those documents, I told you that we're done." He glared at Delgado. "And I told you that I put copies of everything I gave you in a safe place. If anything happens to me, those documents will be given to the authorities."

"I remember. Except I'm thinkin' that the authorities may already have them documents."

"Why do you think that?"

"My high-priced lawyers think you boys have evidence that we don't know about. They say that things are going too well for us, and that Scanlon is no fool. He wouldn't have filed the case on the evidence he's disclosed."

Forest smirked. "You're here, hassling me and jeopardizing both of us, because your lawyers think your case is too good? Now I've heard everything."

Delgado grasped Forest's elbow. "Listen to me, you two-bit addict. Do my lawyers know about everything you've got? Have you given that sissy Scanlon the documents that you retrieved for me?"

The hair stood up on the back of Forest's neck.

"'Cause if you did, the boys will take care of you."

Forest shook his arm free of Delgado's grip and reached across him to open the passenger side door. "Get out. I didn't give Scanlon the copies. Your lawyers know what we know."

"I'm watching you," Delgado said as he got out of Forest's car. "One wrong move, and it'll be over for you."

Forest sat in his car long after Delgado's taillights had disappeared from view. He debated calling Alex but decided it could wait until morning. He couldn't deny it; something about Delgado's tone was more menacing than usual. Forest started his car and headed directly home. His appetite was gone.

———

Delgado's man sat in his car in his usual observation post along the road that ran behind Rosemont. With the leaves off of the trees in winter, the spot afforded him the perfect view of the stately mansion on the hill. His instructions were to keep watch until the occupants—at present, Maggie Martin and John Allen—turned out their lights and presumably went to bed.

The good vet and his wife were early risers and usually turned in well before ten, and he spent the evening playing games on his phone and got home at a decent hour. All in all, this was a cushy gig, and he hoped the trial would drag on for months. He checked the clock on his car dashboard. Another ten minutes, and he would be done for the day.

He frowned when the call came in and he noted the familiar phone number. Delgado was calling from his office. At this time of night, his boss would almost certainly be drunk. He punched the button to accept the call. "Sir," he said.

"They gone to bed yet?"

"No. Should be any minute now."

"Good. When you're done, come by my office. I got another job for you."

"Do you want to tell me about it now? So you don't have to wait for me?" he said, hoping that Delgado would spare him the trip to his sleazy quarters. The man had worked for some questionable characters in his time, but there was an undercurrent of evil in Delgado that he'd never encountered before. These late-night private meetings with his boss unnerved even him.

"Just get here as soon as you're done." Delgado disconnected the call.

The light on the second floor of the house above him went out. He sighed and turned his car toward D's Liquor and Convenience Store. Delgado hadn't sounded drunk and if he hurried, he might find him still sober. That would make a nice change.

Delgado opened the office door before his associate had even reached the top step. He pushed the man in and locked the door behind him. A shadow swept over his face, and Delgado attempted a smile. "I got enemies in this town. Can't be too careful. The police are always sayin' to lock your doors. I'm just bein' a law-abiding citizen and taking their advice." He chuckled at his own joke.

He ensconced himself behind his desk and motioned for the man to sit across from him. He wanted this over quick. An empty glass and an unopened bottle of whiskey on his desk were calling his name, but he needed to have full control of his faculties for this conversation.

"I've got a job for you. An important job."

The man nodded.

Delgado heaved himself forward in his chair and leaned his forearms on his desk. "You know that Forest Smith kid? The lawyer that's assisting that sissy Scanlon on the case against me?"

He nodded again.

"We own him." Delgado chuckled. "Or at least we thought we did."

"How so?"

"He's an addict. We found out and threatened to go to his law firm with it. He's been a highflier there and is on the verge of partnership. We could spoil all that for him." Delgado leaned back in his chair, inspecting the empty glass in his hand. "We convinced him to remove certain records from the documents in the state's file against me and share them with us."

"He did that?"

"Yep. Except he says he kept copies for himself, as insurance. Said he's done with us." Delgado spit at a smudge on the glass and rubbed it against his grease-stained shirt. "Frankly, I don't think he's keeping his promise to us."

"Why do you say that?"

"My lawyer thinks they've got more evidence against me than we know about or they wouldn't have indicted me. Which would mean this Smith kid is hiding something from me."

"Want me to talk to him? Remind him of his obligation to you?"

Delgado shook his head. "I already did that. Tonight. And I don't like how the conversation went."

"He didn't admit to double-crossing you, did he?"

"Course not. He denied doin' anything with the evidence that he stole from the state except give it to me. But I know people—know when they're lying. And that kid is lying."

"So what do you want to do about it?"

"I'm tired of worrying about him. It's time for him to go—permanently."

"What are you suggesting?"

"Whaddaya think? Take him out. Your choice how. Suspicious accident—overdose—or a bullet to the brain."

"Don't you think that will make things worse for you? All of a sudden, the assistant prosecutor is killed?"

"Not if you make it look like suicide. He's an addict. He has an accidental overdose, or he finally succumbs to the shame of his addiction. I don't care how you do it. Just do it in a way that won't lead back to me."

The man was shaking his head. "No. Not this time."

Delgado slammed his fist on the desk. "Whaddaya mean, no? You do what I say you do."

"Not this. I'm not going to murder an assistant prosecutor. This is crazy. Did you talk to your lawyer about it?"

"What are you—stupid? Of course, I didn't talk to him about it! Even a mob lawyer won't advise you to commit murder." Delgado raised his voice to a shout. "I'm telling you to get this done—NOW!"

"And I'm telling you I won't do it!" the man shouted back, rising to his feet. He turned and walked toward the door. Delgado followed him. "If you want Forest Smith dead," he muttered, "you'll have to do it yourself. That is"—he turned and locked eyes with Delgado—"if you still have the balls."

"I still have the balls," Delgado said, his voice gruff. "You might find out for yourself, one day. Now get the hell out of my office." He reached around the man and unlocked the door. "Go back to work, and keep your trap shut." On this last syllable, spit flew out of Delgado's mouth and landed on the man's cheek. He leaned in, his breath hot and stale. "Don't cross me again, buddy boy, or you'll learn things you don't want to know.

Chapter 12

Chuck Delgado slammed himself into his desk chair, grabbed the bottle of Jameson, and twisted off the cap. Someone in his employ had actually refused a direct order. His hand shook as he filled a glass with the amber liquid, but stopped himself before taking a sip. There'd be time for a drink later. He needed to be clearheaded now.

He wrenched open the middle desk drawer and pulled out the false bottom to reveal the slim black notebook of phone numbers he kept for just such a situation. Delgado thumbed through the pages, then tossed the book back into the drawer. He wasn't sure he could count on any of them. Ever since his arrest, his network had been shrinking. *All running for cover,* he thought. *Thinkin' old Chuck Delgado was done for—out of the game.*

He leaned back and grinned mirthlessly. Back in his prime, no one would have dared to refuse a request from Chuck Delgado. They'd have been honored just to have been asked. His name had struck fear in his enemies and in his circle of associates.

Delgado went to the safe that stood in the corner of his office and spun the combination. He slid aside the stacks of bills he kept handy—in case of an emergency—and removed the gun and box of ammunition. Maybe it was time to show the world that he still had what it took. If Smith turned up dead, that good-for-nothing wiseguy would know who did it and word would spread through his network like wildfire. The gun wasn't registered—they'd never be able to trace a bullet to him.

Delgado inserted a clip in the gun and moved to his filing cabinet. He'd had Smith followed and had a file on his daily routine. He retrieved the file marked "F.S." and settled onto his sofa to read.

Delgado opened one bleary eye when the alarm on his watch went off at five o'clock the next morning. He normally didn't get up this early, but he had things to take care of. He'd learned that Forest Smith was an avid runner, going out every morning—rain or shine—between five thirty and six. He did a four-mile run on one of three routes. His time wasn't half bad, Delgado noted. The guy was in good shape.

He'd formulated his plan shortly after midnight. Forest usually ran along the country road that skirted the back lawn of Rosemont, veering off the highway through dense woods and across a two-lane bridge over a deep ravine. Delgado knew that area well. In the early pre-dawn hours, his car would be shielded by the dense growth of trees at the eastern edge of the bridge. He'd wait until Smith was halfway across the bridge and then he'd step out of the shadows and shoot. He smiled to himself. He could just imagine the look on that smug kid's face when he realized he'd underestimated Chuck Delgado.

Delgado went into the bathroom and splashed water onto his face. He checked the clip on his gun, then donned his heavy overcoat and placed the gun in the right-hand pocket.

He crept quietly down the stairs and got into his car. With any luck, Smith would be running the Rosemont route this morning and Delgado could finish his business and be back in his office before the store opened at nine.

———

Forest Smith groaned when his alarm went off at five o'clock. He reached for the snooze button but stopped himself at the last minute. Running was his stress reliever, his salvation. After last night's confrontation with Delgado, he needed to run.

He propelled himself out of bed and threw on the warm running clothes and the shoes he'd placed in their usual spot the night before. It had been an unusually warm February, but a cold front was coming. Freezing rain and snow for the rest of the week, according to the forecast. He peered out the blinds and smiled at his good fortune. The weather was clear and the pavement still dry, which meant he could take his favorite route for at least another day. That bridge would be dangerous once the weather hit.

Forest stepped outside his back door and stretched. Feeling better now that he was outside and moving, he took off. The pavement was dark as the heavy clouds covered the waning moon, and the sun had not yet broken the horizon. The path was seared in his mind, however, and Smith ran at a brisk clip, feeling better with each footfall.

He was breathing hard, enjoying the rhythm of his feet hitting the pavement when he reached the bridge. Head down, concentrating on the road, he didn't see the dark figure emerge from the shadows. He was only forty feet away when he heard Delgado call his name. Forest looked up in time to see Delgado level the gun at him.

He stopped and held up both hands. "You don't want to do this," he began.

"Oh, but I do," Delgado said. "You see, I don't believe you kept your promise. And I don't tolerate people who break promises to me."

"You won't get away with this." Forest took a few slow steps backward on the bridge.

"I think I will," Delgado replied. "I just wanted to see your face when you realized who you're dealing with, you lying sack of shit."

Forest took another step back and bumped up against the railing.

"Careful, now," Delgado said. "You wouldn't want to fall." He pulled the trigger, and the crack of the shot reverberated in the stillness. Forest recoiled. His back hit the barricade and his arms flew up, then he was sailing over the top of the barricade and falling into the creek at the base of the ravine, landing with a terrible crack.

Delgado looked around to make sure he was still alone, then crossed to the railing and looked down. Forest Smith's body lay sprawled out on the rocks, his limbs twisted at improbable angles. His eyes were open and sightless. Delgado stared at the body, searching for a growing red stain but none appeared. Was it possible that he'd missed and the bastard had fallen to his death?

Delgado smirked and quickly returned to his car. He drove directly to his office, taking care to remain within the speed limit. The last thing he needed was to be pulled over by the cops. It was seven twenty when he climbed the stairs and let himself into his office. He'd achieved his purpose. Smith was dead, and no one had seen him come or go. He replaced his gun in the back of his safe and poured himself a tumbler of Jameson.

John Allen removed his down jacket from the coat rack in the kitchen and whistled for the dogs.

Maggie was seated at the counter with a cup of coffee and the morning paper. "Where are you headed?" she asked.

"This may be the last warm day for quite a while. I thought I'd take the dogs for a walk."

"Good idea," Maggie nodded.

"Want to come with us? You know it'll be good for you and you'll be relegated to the treadmill once the weather breaks. You know how bored you get with the treadmill."

Maggie folded the paper and put it on the counter.

"Plus, you'd be keeping me company, and I always love that."

She flashed him a brilliant smile. "Me, too. This may be another busy week at Town Hall, so we'd better spend time together when we can. Let me get my shoes."

Maggie reentered the kitchen wearing her walking shoes and heavy jacket as John finished securing the leashes on Eve and Roman. He handed Maggie the leash for the terrier mix that had brought them together. Eve had adopted her on her first night at Rosemont. She was the reason Maggie had come to Westbury Animal Hospital. Without Eve, Maggie and John might never have met, and she was eternally grateful to the unruly but charming creature.

"Where to?" she asked as they stepped out the door.

"If you have time, let's walk along the road below Rosemont and over to the ravine. It'll take forty-five minutes for us to get over the bridge and back. What do you say?"

Maggie looked at her watch. "It's almost eight, and I don't have anything on my calendar until eleven. Let's go for it."

They set off, the dogs trotting at their heels. "It's unusual for you to be going to the animal hospital so late."

"That young vet I hired is doing a great job. I've decided to take myself off the schedule one morning a week."

"It's about time. You work yourself way too hard."

"Said the pot to the kettle," John replied and slipped his free arm around his wife's waist.

They walked in silence, enjoying the still morning. The dogs sniffed the air and kept pace until they reached the entrance to the bridge. Roman began to bark, a deep throaty explosion of sound. Eve growled menacingly.

"What in the world?" Maggie asked.

Roman pulled and strained at the end of his leash. John ordered the dog to heel, to no avail. "This isn't like him at all," John said, turning to Maggie. "Stay here with Eve."

Maggie knelt down and grasped the collar of her squirming dog.

"I'm going to let Roman lead me to whatever's agitating him."

"Is it safe?"

"I'm sure it's probably just a dead animal or something. Maybe a dog got hit by a car. Let me investigate."

Maggie nodded and kept her eyes trained on him as he followed Roman, thrashing and straining, to the middle of the bridge. She watched as he leaned over the railing and then quickly brought his hand to his heart. He turned toward her, and although his face was in shadow, she could tell from the set of his shoulders that something was terribly wrong.

"Did you bring your cell?" he called.

She nodded vigorously.

"Call the police. We've got a dead body in the ravine."

Maggie gasped. "Are you sure they're dead? Shouldn't we go check?"

John shook his head. "He's dead."

She pulled out her cell phone and placed the call. "They said to wait until they get here," she said as she disconnected the call.

John rejoined her and commanded Roman to lie down.

"Who is it, do you know?"

John turned to her, his expression grave. "Forest Smith. Your assistant prosecutor is dead at the bottom of that ravine."

Chapter 13

David Wheeler turned at the sound of his name and found himself facing Grace Acosta. Her cheeks were rosy, and even with a runny nose, she was pretty.

"I thought I was going to be late for school," Grace said, slightly out of breath.

"I know. It sounds like some sort of accident happened on the other side of town. A bunch of police and emergency vehicles messed up traffic."

She checked the large clock in the hallway. "We've got four minutes. We'll be fine."

"Other than first period math, I don't see you around much. How's it going?"

She flashed her thousand-watt smile. "Great. I got a part in the school musical."

"Congratulations. What is it?"

"*Into the Woods*. Do you know it?"

David shook his head.

"Then you'll have to come see it. It's a Stephen Sondheim classic. Sort of edgy and dark, but the teacher is cutting most of that stuff out." She pushed her hair behind her ears. "I'm Cinderella."

David furrowed his brow. "I thought Cinderella was its own story."

Grace laughed. "It is, but she's also a character in this play."

"I see," David fibbed, realizing he'd have to take her word for it until he saw the show. "So how's Tommy doing?"

"He's great. His eyes are fine, and he likes his new school. He's driving our poor old dog crazy."

"The corgi? Why?"

"She's ancient, and all Tommy wants to do when he gets home from school is chase her around the house. Mom keeps telling him he'll give her a heart attack, but he won't listen."

"Maybe you should get another dog?"

"We've thought of that. But Tommy says he wants a cat."

"Cats are cool. I have a cat," David said, thinking of Namor.

"Mom's worried that our dog won't get along with a cat, and we'll have to get rid of it. But Tommy's birthday is this weekend, so Dad thinks we should just get one from the pet store and hope for the best."

"I've got a better idea," David said. "We've got cats at Forever Friends, and I know which ones are sociable and get along with dogs. Why don't I pick one out that I think Tommy will like and bring it by your house? If he doesn't like the cat—or your corgi objects—I'll bring 'em right back to the shelter."

"You could do that? That would be super."

David nodded.

"Can you bring the cat over at four on Saturday? He's having a few of his friends over for pizza and a movie night. The kids get there at five, so he'd have time to get to know the cat before they arrive."

"Sure, but you'd better check with your Mom to see if this is okay with her. If it's not, you can text me."

Grace handed him her phone, and David punched in his number. "Can you stay for pizza, too? Keep me company."

David nodded as they slid into their seats in math class—just seconds before the bell rang.

Frank Haynes was unlocking the door to Haynes Enterprises when six police cars sped by on the road at the end of the parking lot, sirens blaring and lights flashing. He turned to stare after them. He couldn't remember the last time he'd seen that kind of police response in Westbury. He opened the door and was stepping inside when two ambulances and a fire truck followed in the wake of the police cars. Something was definitely wrong.

He logged in to his computer and went to the *Westbury Gazette* website. He wanted to see if they'd posted anything that would explain what he'd just seen but came up empty-handed.

The outer office door opened, and Loretta hurried in. "Sorry I'm late, Frank. Part of my route was blocked by the police. They made us all turn around and double back. It took forever." She came to stand by his desk.

"A whole string of police cars screamed by here earlier, followed by two ambulances and a fire truck. I was just checking to see if there was anything online about it."

"Whatever it is," Loretta said, "it seems pretty important. I guess we'll find out later."

Frank nodded. "In the meantime, I'm going to work on cash projections for next week."

"I'll bring you a cup of coffee," Loretta said as more sirens could be heard in the distance.

"Thanks. And hold my calls. I'll need to concentrate on the numbers."

<hr />

The black sedan with the darkly tinted windows pulled to the shoulder of the road to allow a string of police and emergency vehicles to pass. Something big had definitely happened. He thought about making a U-turn and following them but decided against it. If it were anything important, he'd hear about it later. Right now, he needed to proceed to his usual surveillance spot at Haynes Enterprises. After his conversation with Delgado last night, he didn't want to do anything that would unhinge his boss.

<hr />

Loretta tapped lightly on the door to Frank's office. He tore his eyes from the spreadsheets strewn across his desk. "Can this wait?" he asked. "I'm in the middle—"

She shook her head, pointing to the phone. "It's Maggie—Mayor Martin," she corrected herself. "Says it's urgent."

Frank rolled his chair to the credenza and picked up the phone. "Maggie. Is this about the police activity earlier?"

"You heard about that?"

"I didn't 'hear about it,' I heard it. They roared right past our office earlier this morning. I searched online to get an explanation but didn't find anything. What happened?"

Maggie drew a deep breath. "There's no easy way to say this. Forest Smith is dead. As a member of the council, you need to know before it hits the news."

Frank gasped. "How? What happened?"

"It looks like he fell off a bridge into the ravine in the wooded area just below Rosemont."

Frank let out a low whistle.

"He died from the fall. Broken neck. The medical examiner says he would have died instantly."

"Poor kid. Did he fall or did he jump?" Frank asked. "It's clear, and the roads aren't icy. What was he doing on the bridge?"

"Apparently, he jogs every morning before work, and it's one of his favorite routes."

"What time did this happen?"

"Best guess is shortly before eight."

"Who found him?"

"John and I."

Frank sucked in his breath. "That must have been horrible. I'm so sorry."

Maggie swallowed hard. "It was. The medical examiner hasn't fixed the cause of death yet. As you say, the roads were clear and it seems very unlikely that he would have fallen off the bridge while jogging. The police have contacted next of kin, and his sister is meeting them at his house. They'll be looking for a suicide note."

Maggie and Frank were both silent. Frank stood and began to pace. "I'm shocked, Maggie. I didn't know the kid very well, but he had a lot on the ball and didn't seem like a candidate for suicide to me."

"I agree," Maggie said. "So does Alex."

"How's he holding up?"

"Devastated, Frank. You can imagine."

"This would make two suicides—two men in the prime of their lives—connected to this case. Seems like too much of a coincidence to me."

"That's the way it strikes Alex and me, too. And Delgado is capable of anything."

Frank raked his fingers through his hair. "For God's sake, Maggie, be careful."

"You too, Frank," she said. "We'll be holding a press conference at four. We're hoping the medical examiner can establish the cause of death by then. I'd like you to be there, Frank. We need to present a united front within town government."

"I'll be there. You can count on me."

"Thank you, Frank. See you then."

Frank's hand shook as he replaced the receiver into its cradle.

Loretta, who had stationed herself just outside of his open doorway, now stepped into his office.

"I heard most of that," she said, not attempting to hide her eavesdropping. "Someone's dead?"

Frank took her hands in his and led her to the sofa and looked into her eyes.

"A young attorney, Forest Smith, fell to his death in a ravine below Maggie's house this morning. That's where all the police cars were headed."

Loretta rocked back in her seat. "He's helping Alex on the case against Delgado?"

"He was helping, yes. They're saying it looks like suicide."

"You don't believe that, do you? Maggie doesn't, either?"

Frank nodded.

"You think it's murder? Delgado murdered Forest Smith?"

"I'd bet my last dollar." He leaned toward her. "Delgado is a monster. You and the kids need to stay away from him."

Loretta nodded. "You don't need to worry about that, Frank. I'm concerned about you. You're in danger too," she said, remembering the jump drive hidden in her closet. The one she'd taken from Frank's safe and copied, that contained names and account numbers she felt certain related to the fraud and embezzlement case Forest Smith had been working on.

Frank cocked his head. "Why do you say that?"

Loretta swallowed hard. She wondered what Frank would think of her if he knew she'd snooped in his safe and stolen his confidential data. "You used to be on the town council together," she said, recovering herself.

Frank released her hands and sighed. "I guess you're right about that. I'm not worried about me. I can take care of myself."

She reached for his face and laid a gentle kiss on his forehead. "That's probably what Forest Smith thought, too."

Chapter 14

Maggie Martin stepped to the podium set up in the lobby of Town Hall. "Good afternoon. It is with great sadness that we've gathered you here today. As some of you may know, the body of local attorney Forest Smith was found this morning along a tributary of the Shawnee River. He died from injuries sustained in a fall likely from a bridge near where his body was found. Mr. Smith was an attorney at the law firm of Stetson and Graham and was assisting Special Counsel Alex Scanlon in the case against former Councilmember Charles Delgado. He is survived by his parents and his two sisters. Our deepest condolences go out to his family at this sad time. Visitation will be tomorrow night at Sanger's Funeral Home, and a memorial service celebrating his life will be held Saturday at eleven o'clock at First Methodist Church."

Maggie placed the written statement on the podium and removed her reading glasses. John was leaning against the wall on the far side of the lobby behind the crowd. He nodded to her, and she felt the surge of calm she always felt in his presence. Hands shot up in the sea of reporters in front of her. She recognized a few locals, but there were many faces she didn't know. Word spread fast, and it appeared everyone had the same suspicions she had. She pointed to a woman in the back row.

"Were there any witnesses to Mr. Smith's fall?"

Maggie turned to Chief Thomas, who stepped to the microphone. "None have come forward."

"Are there any signs of foul play?" a man shouted the question.

Chief Thomas shook his head. "The area is still under investigation, but we haven't uncovered anything of relevance at this time."

"Could this be a suicide?"

Alex stepped forward. "No note has been found. As Forest's colleague and friend," his voice cracked and he swallowed hard, "I do not believe he committed suicide."

"So, he either slipped off dry pavement or someone pushed him," stated a man in the front row.

Chief Thomas leaned toward the microphone. "That's all the information we have at this time. We'll let you know of any developments as our investigation continues. Thank you."

Frank Haynes stepped forward and touched Maggie's elbow. "We should get out of here, fast," he said.

Tonya Holmes was on the other side of her. "I agree with Frank. Let's go."

Maggie turned and proceeded to the elevator bank, Alex and the chief behind her. "Wait," Maggie said. "John's out there."

"You go on, and I'll find him," Tonya said. "Tim Knudsen just texted me, and he'll be here shortly. He got held up in a closing."

"Let's convene in my office in ten minutes to figure out what we're going to do now," Maggie said as she stepped onto the elevator.

———

Chuck Delgado pushed the off button on his television remote and reached for his bottle of Jameson. This kind of good news called for a celebration. Smith had died from injuries from the fall. What a stroke of luck. If they'd found a bullet in the bastard, they would have called it murder. And they would have found a bullet by now.

He poured himself a double and leaned back in his chair, putting his feet on his desk. A frown settled on his face. His shot must have gone wide, missing Smith. How long had it been since he'd fired a gun? He couldn't remember the last time. It wasn't good to be rusty, especially now. He might need this particular skill again—soon.

Delgado took a generous drink from his glass and swirled the amber liquid around his mouth. He'd make time for target practice.

———

Maggie, John, Chief Thomas, and Councilmembers Holmes, Haynes, and Knudsen were seated at the conference table in Maggie's office. Alex paced in front of the windows. Town Hall had closed and the throng of reporters had set up camp on the front steps.

Alex separated the blinds with his fingers and peered out. Television news vans with raised antennae towers lined the curb next to the building. "They're not buying our story that this was an accidental death," he said.

"It may not be," Chief Thomas replied, "but we don't have one scrap of evidence to indicate it was murder, much less anything to implicate a perpetrator."

"Just because there wasn't a note, it doesn't rule out suicide," Tim said. "Smith was under a lot of pressure, and he was a recovering addict. Maybe everything became too much to cope with."

Alex rounded on him. "That's not what happened. Forest was fine and doing a great job on the case. If he was suicidal, I would have noticed."

"No one's faulting you for any of this, Alex," Maggie said. "Where do we go from here, Chief?"

"I know this isn't what you want to hear, but we wait for the results of the investigation. Something might turn up at the scene."

"That wooded area is an awfully big, messy crime scene," Frank said. "Won't it be impossible to search?"

The chief nodded. "Difficult but not impossible. That's why we need time."

John leaned forward and rested his forearms on the table. "Whether you can ever prove foul play or not," he said, "I'm convinced that Forest was murdered. By Delgado or one of his henchmen. That leaves all of you at risk." John turned to Chief Thomas. "What are you going to do to keep everyone here safe?"

"Maggie and Alex are the ones at risk," Frank said.

Tonya and Tim nodded their agreement.

"We've already got security details on your homes," the chief said.

"You had a security detail on Forest Smith, too, didn't you?" John asked, slapping the table with his palm. "Some good that did him."

Maggie leaned forward. "Forest's death isn't the chief's fault."

"I agree with your husband, Maggie. We should have protected Smith." The chief ran his hand over his eyes. "I've already authorized overtime and doubled your security details. In the meantime, let me know, personally, if you are going anywhere other than your homes or offices." He held up his cell phone. "You both have my number?"

Maggie and Alex nodded.

"Let's all keep our eyes and ears open, and don't take any unnecessary risks. If this is murder, we're going to find who did it."

Delgado's man placed his cell phone on the dashboard of his car. The press conference at Town Hall had been live streamed, and he'd watched all of it. He sank back against the seat. Forest Smith was dead, and the authorities thought it was an accident or suicide. He took a long drag on his cigarette, then rolled down his automatic window and flicked the butt onto the pavement where it smoldered and went dark.

Not likely, he thought. Delgado was behind this. He'd probably convinced someone else to do the dirty deed for him. Surely Delgado didn't have the stones to do it himself. Especially not in a way that couldn't be easily identified as murder. If Delgado was going to kill someone, he'd shoot them. Anything else would require too much muscle and too much finesse, both of which were in short supply in the man referred to as "the troll" in certain circles.

An involuntary shiver ran down his spine. What if he'd underestimated Delgado? What if he was capable of such an act? It was time for him to make some judicious inquiries. If anyone knew who killed Forest Smith, he would find out.

"Let's stay in tonight. Do you mind?" Maggie asked as John pulled into the garage at Rosemont.

John unlocked the back door, where they were greeted by the effusive Eve. Roman hung back, head down.

"Come here, boy," John said, kneeling down and massaging the golden retriever's ears, working his way down his back to his tail bone.

"I think he's freaked out about finding Forest's body this morning," Maggie said.

"You may be right. Animals are far more intuitive than we give them credit for."

"Will he be okay?"

"Sure. But I'm glad we're staying home. He needs our company. Why don't I do the cooking tonight?"

Maggie raised an eyebrow. "And what would that be?"

"I was planning to order a pizza. That counts, doesn't it?"

Maggie moved Eve's paws from her thighs and leaned over to kiss the top of John's head. "Sounds perfect. I don't care what we have as long as I can go upstairs and put my pajamas on."

John held up his keys, pantomiming a microphone, and asked the dogs, "What's the deal with women and pajamas?" then turned to Maggie, "I can't remember ever getting ready for bed before seven in the evening."

Maggie gave an exaggerated eye roll. "Don't knock it till you've tried it, Mr. Comedian. I'm going to call Susan. She needs to hear about Forest, and I want her to hear it from me."

Chapter 15

Susan picked up the phone on her desk. "Your mother is on the line, Mrs. Scanlon." Susan smiled; she loved being called Mrs. Scanlon.

"Hi, Mom. What's up?"

"I know you're at work, so I'll keep this brief." Maggie drew a deep breath and continued. "Forest Smith was found dead this morning."

"What?" Susan gasped. "What in the world happened?"

Maggie supplied what she knew about the tragedy. When she finished, both women remained silent while Susan took it all in.

"It's got to be murder, don't you think? What does Alex have to say about it?"

"Our public stance is that we're waiting for the police to finish their investigation, but privately, we agree with you."

"This terrifies me for both of you, Mom. Are the police giving you protection?"

"They are, honey. You've got nothing to worry about. We'll be fine. We just need to redouble our efforts to get Delgado off the streets."

"I agree."

"How are you feeling? You're still at work; I thought you were only going to do half-days for the next month or so."

"I'm working in the afternoons. Mornings are difficult for me. I'm queasy, and it's hard for me to get going. I've been getting up at ten and coming into the office by noon."

"What does Aaron say about that?"

"He says it's normal, and it's just going to take time to get my stamina back."

"He's the doctor, so he should know."

"Aaron is pampering me like crazy; I don't have to lift a finger at home. And he's bringing me flowers every other day. I'm running out of places to put them."

"Glad to hear it. That's exactly as it should be. You married the right guy, honey." Maggie held the phone away from her ear and sniffed the air.

"I think our pizza just arrived. I'm going to go eat while it's hot. Give that handsome husband of yours a hug from me."

"Will do. And call me the minute you hear anything else about Forest's death."

———

Susan texted her husband with a brief summary of the shocking news about Forest Smith. Aaron immediately called her.

"I just ducked out of a patient's room," he said. "Can you call Alex? I'm going to be tied up at the hospital for three or four more hours."

"Of course." She paused. "So, you won't be home for dinner?"

"Not tonight, sweetheart. I'm sorry. But I've got the weekend off. Why don't we go to a matinee movie on Saturday and then get something to eat? Will you feel good enough for that?"

"I will indeed," she replied. "And if you're leaving the choice up to me, we'll be seeing a romantic comedy."

"Whatever you want."

"I like the sound of that. You go back to your patient, and I'll track down that brother of yours."

———

Alex recognized the name on his cell and picked up. "Susan. You heard?"

"Mom just told me."

"Then you'll know everything we know. I don't have anything to add."

"He was a good friend in addition to a colleague, wasn't he? This must be heartbreaking for you. I'm very sorry, Alex."

"We've got to get this monster Delgado behind bars." Alex choked on the words. "I owe this to Forest and to the public."

"Has Stetson and Graham assigned a replacement for Forest?"

"Not yet. I think they're still in shock, like the rest of us."

Susan tapped her finger on her desk. "You're still at your office, aren't you? Working extra hard and not giving yourself a chance to grieve?"

Alex remained silent.

"Thought so. Here's what we're going to do. I'm going to continue to assist you. Send me anything and everything you need help with."

"You can't do that, Susan. You've got your own case load, and Aaron says that your recovery is slow. Not to mention the fact that I don't have any money in the budget to pay you."

"My firm has a strong commitment to pro bono work," Susan said. "I'll log my hours that way. Don't worry about the paperwork on my end; I'll handle that." She glanced at her watch. "It's almost five. Send me something before I leave here in twenty minutes, and I'll work on it at home tonight."

"You're a lifesaver, Susan. My brother knew what he was doing when he married you."

⁂

Maggie and Eve cuddled in a corner of the sofa, watching *Downton Abbey* on DVD. Blossom, Buttercup, and Bubbles were huddled in a clump on the hearth rug. "It never gets old, does it? No matter how many times I watch an episode, I still see something new."

John smiled at his bride. "This show is your happy place, isn't it?"

"Mine and millions of other people's. Admit it, John Allen, you love it too."

"Don't tell anyone, but I do." He rose from the other end of the sofa, taking care not to disturb Roman who was snoring lightly at his feet.

"I think it's soothing for Roman," Maggie said.

"You may be right. I'll be right back. I'm going to get the mail."

"Do you want me to pause it?" she asked, picking up the remote.

John shook his head. "I'll only be a minute."

He stepped out of the room and returned before the scene changed. He held out an envelope to her. "Something for you from Highpointe College," he said. "The rest was junk mail."

Maggie paused the show and opened the slim envelope bearing the return address of the president of the college. She quickly read the letter, looked up at John, and then read the contents aloud.

"Thank you for your recent participation in our Careers of the Future panel discussion. Professor Acosta told me that your presentation was superb. The reviews we've received from the students in attendance have been extremely positive. I want to discuss a more robust affiliation with the college, perhaps on one of our advisory boards, and would like to invite you to lunch at your convenience."

Maggie dropped the letter to her lap. "What a nice thing to say to me," she said, a bit breathless. "I had such a good time with the students, but I never imagined I had this sort of impact."

"It doesn't surprise me at all, my dear."

"I don't have time for anything else right now," she added quickly. "This is ridiculous. It's out of the question. I'll send him an email thanking him but telling him I'm too busy."

"Don't do that. Have lunch with the man. Find out what he's proposing." John leaned over and took the letter from her and re-read it. "This is quite an honor. You love being on a college campus; you were glowing when you came home after the panel. This could be fun, and you owe it to yourself to find out what he has in mind."

Chapter 16

David opened the rear passenger door and stowed the cat carrier on the floor. He climbed into the front seat next to Grace. "Sorry I made you wait," he said. "We got busy this afternoon."

"No problem." Grace smiled at him and then backed out of the parking spot, where she'd been watching prospective pet owners going in and out of Forever Friends for the last twenty minutes or so. "I'm just glad that you found a cat for Tommy."

"He's a dandy," David said, turning to look back at the carrier. "Very playful and funny, and very friendly. He loves attention and will curl up next to you for hours."

"That's exactly what Tommy wants. Now if our dog likes him, we're all set."

"Is Tommy excited?"

"Mom and Dad decided not to tell him. They're big on surprises." She glanced over at him. "Every year, they throw surprise parties for us and each other. We're not really surprised anymore, but it makes them happy."

"Do you like surprises?"

"Not so much. I'd rather have the fun of anticipation."

David considered this. "No one's ever thrown a surprise party in my family, so I guess I don't know what I'd prefer."

"Did your parents do a lot of entertaining when you were a kid?"

"My dad was the life of the party. People flocked to him. He was always inviting people over. My mom is shy and keeps to herself. Especially now, after my dad died."

Grace put on her blinker and turned onto a residential street lined with imposing brick homes set far from traffic. Deep lawns were studded with mature trees waiting to spread their green canopy in spring. She pulled into the third driveway on the right, opened the garage door, and parked the car.

"He's awfully quiet in there," Grace remarked as David tucked the cat carrier under his arm. "How should we go about this?"

"Can you put your dog in another room when I bring the cat in the house? Maybe we can take the cat to Tommy's room to meet Tommy first, and then the two animals can sniff each other under the door. We'll take it from there."

Grace nodded. "I told Mom you'd know what to do."

"I'm no expert."

"That's not what Frank Haynes told us that day we met at the park. He said you're brilliant with animals, that you have a sixth sense. He said you're thinking of becoming a vet."

David's face turned a deep scarlet. He was grateful when the cat started to yowl. "Let's get him inside," David said.

Grace opened the door and walked quietly down the hallway, motioning for David to stay back. She turned a corner and disappeared from sight, then quickly returned. "Tommy's in the living room watching a show he likes. Let's take the cat to his room. Mom will send him up to change for the party as soon as the show is over."

David followed Grace to Tommy's room. He placed the carrier on the floor and opened it after she closed the door. Sitting next to it, he motioned for Grace to join him. "He'll come out when he's ready."

The cat began to meow, softly at first and then with increasing volume. One cautious gray paw appeared outside the carrier, followed by another. They watched the cat grow comfortable with its surroundings, pouncing on sunbeams on the floor and leaping from the bed to the top of the dresser and back.

"What're you doin' in my room?" Tommy said, opening the door to find his sister sitting on the floor.

"Hi, Tommy," David said from the other side of the room.

Tommy spun around to face David. "Hey, David," he said, confused. "How come you're here?"

"Your family had me bring you something for your birthday," he said, scooping the cat out of the clothes hamper where he'd stashed it when they heard Tommy opening the door. He held out the squirming gray fur ball to David. "What do you think?"

"Is he for me?" Tommy gathered the creature into his arms. He turned to his sister. "Mom said we'd think about it. That always means no."

Grace laughed and tousled his hair. "Not this time, it didn't."

"Go get your dog," David said to Grace. "We'll introduce them, and if all goes well, I think you've got a new cat."

———

Kevin Acosta tapped on the bedroom door fifteen minutes later. David and Grace were sitting on the floor, backs against the bed, their legs stretched out in front of them, discussing the impossibility of this week's math homework. Tommy lay on his bed, reading a comic book, with the corgi pressed to his right side and the cat curled into a ball on his left. "Isn't this the tranquil scene? Who's your new friend?" Kevin asked, pointing to the cat.

Tommy looked up at his father. "I'm calling him Magellan," he said. "Like the explorer."

"That's a very learned name," Kevin said, nodding in approval.

"We can call him Mags for short," Grace chimed in.

"That is, if Mom will let me keep him." Tommy raised hopeful eyes to his father.

"Your mother's only condition was that the cat got along with our dog." Kevin pointed to the sleeping corgi. "I think we've answered that question in the affirmative."

Tommy lunged at his father and hugged him.

"It's time to come downstairs. Your classmates will be here any minute."

Tommy tore out of his room and down the stairs.

"Do you have a litter box?" David asked, looking around the room.

Kevin brought his hand to his forehead. "I'm afraid we didn't think about any of that. We've been so busy getting this party together." He pulled a credit card out of this wallet and handed it to his daughter. "Can the two of you nip out to the pet store and buy whatever's needed for a cat?" he asked sheepishly. "Do you know what we'll need, David?"

"I do. There's not a whole lot, really."

"It's Tommy's birthday, so don't scrimp," Kevin said. "And when you get back, can you stay for the party? Tommy's been talking nonstop to his friends about you and Dodger. You're something of a celebrity around here."

David began to shake his head. "I dunno ..."

"Say yes, please." Grace flashed her smile at him. "Otherwise, I'll spend my whole evening with ten-year-olds. Maybe we can work on our math homework? I've got play rehearsal all day tomorrow, so this may be my only chance."

"Sure," David said, hoping they wouldn't spend all evening doing homework.

Chapter 17

The bartender noticed the telltale tobacco scent even before he spotted the man waiting quietly in the shadows at the end of the bar. He finished pouring a shot and slid it across the bar to a patron on the other side. "Last call, Donny. Drink up. Time to go home."

Donny waved a hand in the air while he downed the liquid. He laid a twenty on the bar and shoved himself off the barstool. "See you tomorrow," he slurred and staggered out the door.

"You didn't take his keys," the man said. "The boss wouldn't like that."

"He don't got no keys. Wife took the car away from him years ago. He takes a cab. Guy's waiting for him now." He gestured to the door. "See for yourself."

The man stepped to the door and locked it.

"You want Delgado's cut?" the bartender asked. "You're not supposed to collect until tomorrow night."

"I'll be back," he said, pulling on his cigarette. "I wanted to talk with you in private."

The bartender stopped wiping the counter and looked at the man. "Yeah?"

"Heard any talk about this Smith kid?"

"The one they found at the bottom of the ravine?"

"That's the one."

"They found a bullet lying on the bridge. It was on the late news. They're not sure if it's related or not. They're still calling it a suicide."

"I don't believe that, do you? Too convenient. Any talk about somebody hired to do the hit? Anybody flashing around some extra cash?"

"I ain't heard nuthin'. If one of the local boy's done the job, I'd of heard of it. Musta been outta Chicago. Or Delgado done it himself."

The man nodded. "Let's keep this talk between us, okay?"

"Sure thing. Whatever you say," the bartender replied.

"I'll be back tomorrow for Delgado's cut. Keep your ear to the ground, and tell me anything you hear."

Delgado parked behind the plumbing supply store next to the bar. This was the night that his flunky collected the protection payments. For a fee, Delgado let most of the mom-and-pop shops do business in the seedier parts of town where he ran his crew. He watched as the man locked his car and went into the bar.

Delgado chuckled to himself as he crossed the parking lot. One of the advantages of providing a "company car" was that he kept a spare key. He popped the trunk, lifted the floor mat, and placed his Glock next to the jack underneath. He shoved the mat back, shut the trunk, and was sliding behind the wheel of his car when he heard the man start the car and pull away.

That idiot police chief and the cartoon cops on the Westbury force got lucky when they found that bullet. It had to be the one he fired at Forest Smith. His aim had gotten bad.

He patted his pocket and pulled out the scrap of paper where he'd written the Silent Witness phone number. The television reporter had urged anyone with information to call. He started his car and headed back to his office. As soon as the man dropped off his payments, Delgado would do his civic duty and call the number. Getting framed for Smith's murder was just what that sissy deserved for refusing to do the deed in the first place.

He was lost in thought as he drove the black sedan along a dark country road back to Delgado's office. Over the last two days, he'd questioned all of his contacts and no one was talking about a hit. "Delgado must have done it himself," he said aloud, "but he's too—" Just then the steering wheel jerked to the right and he felt the car sag. He wrenched the wheel back under his control and cursed as he steered it to the shoulder. He must have blown a tire. The last thing he wanted to do was change a flat at this time of night.

He opened the trunk and slapped at the flashlight whose weak beam quickly petered out and died. Throwing it in the trunk, he reached into the darkness and fumbled for the jack. His hand found a well-machined metal surface, and he stopped short. He knew the feel of a gun. And it wasn't his.

The man rocked back on his heels. The only other person who had a key to this car was Delgado. He took a handkerchief from his pocket and began wiping the gun clean of prints. The time had come for him to turn the tables on Chuck Delgado.

He fixed the flat and drove to the Forest Smith crime scene. The absence of headlights in either direction told him he was alone. He rolled down his car window and flung the gun out the window, sending it sailing over the bridge.

Delgado's man then drove to his apartment and retrieved the spreadsheet he'd found when Delgado had him search the Wheeler home months ago. He smiled to himself. He'd been smart to keep its existence secret from his boss. If that bastard thought he could frame him for Smith's murder, all bets were off. It was time to go to the authorities. Based upon what he'd read in the papers, he'd be able to cut a good deal for himself.

After he left D's Liquor and Convenience Store, he zipped onto the highway. His boss had been drunk when he dropped off the cash. Delgado had barely nodded at the six stacks of bills he'd placed on his desk and was snoring before he'd even closed the door.

Patting the locked glove box where he'd stashed the spreadsheet, he zoomed into the fast lane to pass a long-haul truck up ahead. He was on his way to police headquarters to demand a meeting with the chief and that "sissy Scanlon." He laughed. Oh, to see the look on Delgado's fat face when they nailed him.

He was neck-and-neck with the truck when the driver hit a patch of ice and fishtailed, sending the black sedan with darkly tinted windows across the berm and into a copse of trees. Delgado's man was dead before the truck came to a stop.

Chuck Delgado was awakened from his drunken stupor by the incessant ringing of his phone. He sobered up fast when the voice on the line said a car registered in his name was involved in a fatal accident on the highway and could he please come down to the salvage yard today to remove any personal items from the car?

He heaved himself to his feet and rushed home to shower and shave. He wanted to be at the salvage yard when it opened. With any luck, he'd be able to retrieve the gun, and no one would be the wiser.

When he arrived, the paperwork had taken an eternity and he'd had to control his temper with the officious old woman in charge, but he was finally escorted to his car. The damage made it almost unrecognizable. He shuddered when he looked into the passenger compartment. He made a cursory inspection of it, then managed to pry the trunk open. He found the jack lying loose but no gun. He took a deep breath and methodically searched the trunk. Someone had removed it, and he had no way of knowing who.

He turned and headed back to the trailer that served as the salvage yard office, dazed by the realization that his gun was now missing and the bullet uncovered at the scene of Forest Smith's death was probably a match.

Delgado didn't know what made him turn around, but he retraced his steps to the car. He wasn't able to open either of the front doors, but he managed to dislodge the rear passenger door and crawl into the car. He leaned over the front seat and tried the glove box. It was locked.

He fished the key out of his pants pocket and unlocked it. On top of the registration and owner's manual was a stack of papers from a legal pad, all bearing rows of neat handwritten numbers. He glanced at the numbers on the top sheet and snorted. He recognized them. They were bank accounts belonging to him, his brother, William Wheeler, Russell Isaac, and Frank Haynes. He'd hit the jackpot.

Delgado folded the papers and placed them carefully in his coat pocket. He was whistling when he entered the trailer and signed himself out.

"Didn't you want to take anything with you?" the woman called after him.

Delgado made a dismissive gesture with his hand and kept walking.

Chapter 18

Gloria Vaughn laid her canvas satchel on the glass countertop in Terraces Treasures gift boutique. The pretty young girl manning the register smiled at her. "Can I help you?"

"I'm here to drop off my latest creations," Gloria said. "We sell these in the shop—over there." She pointed to a display hanging to the right of the entrance. Gloria began pulling her wares out of her satchel.

"You made those scarves?" the girl asked. "I've been admiring them since my first day here."

Gloria extended her hand to the girl. "Gloria Harper. And yes—I knitted them."

"Grace Acosta," she said, shaking Gloria's hand.

"I haven't seen you here before, have I?"

Grace shook her head. "I started two weeks ago. My dad's a professor at Highpointe, and we just moved to Westbury."

"Welcome to our town. I've lived here most of my life—and that's a long time." She smiled. "I hope you'll be as happy here as I've been."

Grace picked up one of the scarves that Gloria had removed from her bag. "This one is stunning. It's perfect for my mother. She's got a birthday coming up. Would you mind if I bought it for her? I'll put it aside with a note for my manager, so she can price it. I'll pay for it out of my first paycheck."

"That would give me great pleasure," Gloria said. "I wish I could give you a discount, but the proceeds all go to reduce the mortgage on Fairview Terraces. Our funds were caught up in that mess with the embezzlement, and we're trying to work our way out of it." She looked at her watch. "It's almost lunchtime. Why don't you put the 'Be Right Back' sign on the door and join me for a bite to eat? My treat."

"We're allowed to take breaks," Grace said, "so I guess that would be all right." There was something very comforting about the older woman; Gloria was the personification of the ideal grandmother.

Grace and Gloria were crossing the dining room with their trays when a tall man waved them over to a table in the back of the cafeteria.

"This is my husband, Glenn," Gloria said as the man pulled out a chair for her. She smiled at the young man and his dog standing behind him. "And this is our friend David Wheeler and his dog, Dodger."

Grace and David grinned at each other.

Glenn looked from Grace to David and back again. "You two know each other?"

"We're friends from school," Grace said.

Glenn glanced at David, who was fumbling to hold Grace's chair for her.

While the foursome ate Fairview Terraces' famous "rainy day stew," Grace told them about her brother and the new cat that David had given him. "Mags is perfect for our family. We all love him. We haven't had a cat before, and now I think we'll never be without one."

"You're preaching to the choir," Glenn said. "Gloria and I got a new cat last year—from that litter that Roman found in the woods."

"Namor is from that litter, too," David said. He turned to Grace. "Namor is Roman spelled backwards."

Grace raised a quizzical eyebrow and nodded at David to continue.

"You remember John's dog, Roman? He was missing for days. And Maggie and John put flyers up all over town. They thought he was gone for good, but all the while he was in the woods below Rosemont, protecting a group of kittens whose mother had died. I found them," he said, "and I tried to keep the kittens at my house, but caring for six newborn kittens turns out to be a lot of work. We took them to Rosemont, and Maggie, Sam Torres, and I took turns tending to them. Namor was the most adventurous of the litter. When he was old enough, they let me adopt him."

Grace's smile sparkled. Glenn and Gloria exchanged glances.

"Why don't we leave you two to have some dessert?" Gloria said. "Glenn and I have an appointment."

"I don't remember anything on the calendar ..." Glenn began but stopped in response to the stern look Gloria gave him.

Grace looked at the clock on the wall. "I need to get back to the shop. We're only supposed to close it for short breaks. I've been gone too long already."

"Dodger and I should go back to work, too," David said. "Thanks for lunch, Glenn. See you around, Grace." He nodded to Gloria and made his way out of the dining room. Grace turned to watch him go.

Gloria caught Glenn's eye, then jerked her head in David's direction.

Glenn nodded and followed the boy, dropping into step beside him.

"Very cute girl, that Grace," he said.

"I guess so, yeah."

"She likes you, you know."

"Awww ... c'mon. I don't think so."

They continued to walk in silence.

"Why do you think so?" David asked.

"I've had a long time to learn about people, David," Glenn said. "And after almost eighty years, even women are making sense to me. Trust me— she likes you."

"So what do I do about it?"

"You ask her out on a date. You kids still go on dates, don't you?"

David shrugged. "I guess."

"Ask her to go to the movies and for ice cream afterward. That's a classic first date," the older man advised, warming to his topic. "And make sure it's a movie she'll enjoy. Steer clear of all of those violent films out there these days."

"I don't have a car," David said softly.

"I'll bet your mom will loan you hers. And if she doesn't, you can use mine. Gloria and I stay home in the evenings. It'll be no trouble."

David turned to his friend and smiled. "Thanks, Glenn. You've never steered me wrong. I'll give it a try. I'll ask Grace out when I see her at school next week."

Chapter 19

Phillip Hastings approached the group of reporters gathered on the courthouse steps. The criminal trial of Chuck Delgado was getting a lot of press coverage and Hastings loved being in the limelight. He towered over his client, who stood next to him, hands clasped in front of him. Alex stood to one side, observing the scene. Delgado looked respectable in a well-tailored suit and crisp white shirt. Standing quietly by his lawyer's side, he displayed none of his characteristic swagger.

"We're very pleased with how the case is going," Hastings pontificated. "If this is all the evidence the state has to offer, I don't know why they even brought it to trial. Based upon what we've seen so far, we may move for dismissal before we even present our defense."

A reporter held a microphone out to him. "Wouldn't that be extraordinary to have the case thrown out? Are you that confident?"

"Unheard of, frankly. But in this situation, I think we'll be successful." Hastings spotted Alex and pointed to him.

"There's your special counsel. Ask him if he has any rabbits up his sleeve."

The reporters surged toward Alex.

"You heard him," a reporter for the *Westbury Gazette* yelled. "How does the state feel about its case?"

"As I've told you before, the state does not comment on ongoing litigation." He tried to push his way through the crowd but quickly decided against it and retreated into the courthouse. He flashed his credentials to bypass the security screening and found a private alcove. He removed his phone from his briefcase and placed a call to Maggie.

"I won't make it to your office this afternoon," he said when she answered. "The press is swarming outside, and I'm holed up in the courthouse, waiting for them to leave."

"How did today go?" Maggie asked.

"Watch the news and see Hastings' remarks. He got it right. They're punching holes in everything we've got."

"Don't be discouraged. This is only one day. The case will take months to present."

"Unless we get something else to present, Maggie, it won't matter. Delgado will walk."

"We've got time. Something will turn up."

"From your lips to God's ears. I'll call you tomorrow after I get out of court."

———

Chuck Delgado stepped into the big box electronics store. The judge had recessed the trial an hour earlier than usual, and his attorney said he didn't need to meet with him to go over the day's testimony. He felt like a kid who had gotten out of school early. He browsed through the DVDs. Now that he had to be at the courthouse by eight each morning, he couldn't spend his evenings playing cards and drinking whiskey. He'd buy a movie to watch with his wife, Bertha, and be in bed by nine.

Delgado was on his way to the register with a boxed set of the *Godfather* trilogy when he spotted the display of mini refrigerators. He walked over to inspect a sleek stainless steel model and bought it on the spot. It would look handsome in his office and, based upon the way things were going in court, he'd be spending his days there again soon.

He drove to his convenience store and went in search of the clerk. "I got somethin' in my trunk that needs carryin' upstairs," he said to the older man.

The man, perched on a tall stool behind the counter, swiveled to face Delgado. He raised an eyebrow.

"Don't look at me like that," Delgado retorted. "It's a refrigerator. One of those little office models. I need somebody to carry it to my office."

The man nodded and got up off the stool. "David," he called as he entered the back room.

David came out of the walk-in cooler, wiping his hands on a rag.

Delgado took a step toward the boy. "Who're you?" he asked, peering at him closely.

"David Wheeler, sir," David said, forcing himself to say the word "sir."

"He's been coming in a couple afternoons a week and on Sundays," the older man explained. "He's a real good worker."

"Are you, now?" Delgado said. "How about giving me a hand with something?"

David nodded and followed Delgado to his car. He popped the trunk and began to wrestle with the refrigerator that was lying inside.

"I'll get that, sir," David said, stepping in front of Delgado and picking up the refrigerator without showing any sign of effort. "Where do you want it?" he asked, balancing it on one shoulder.

Delgado gestured with his head to the stairs. "In my office."

David turned and walked effortlessly up the stairs.

Delgado lumbered after him and unlocked the door. "Put it over there—against the wall," he said, pointing.

David carefully lowered the refrigerator into place, then searched for an electrical outlet. He located the nearest one behind a filing cabinet. He pulled open the top drawer to get a handhold on the cabinet.

Delgado rushed over and slammed the drawer shut, almost smashing David's fingers inside. "What do you think you're doing? All them files is private business." He glared at David and pushed the lock into the closed position.

"Sorry, sir. I wasn't looking at the files," David said. "I just wanted to move the cabinet so I could plug your refrigerator into the outlet."

"Find another way," Delgado replied gruffly.

David leaned into the cabinet, using his weight to push it aside. He plugged the refrigerator into the outlet and wrestled the filing cabinet back into place.

Delgado stood behind his desk, watching David. "The wall behind the cabinet's a different color than the rest of the room," he remarked. "I could see that just now."

David nodded. "That's pretty common. Paint can get dirty from cooking oils or tobacco smoke, or even faded by the sun."

"Is that right? How's a kid like you know that?"

"I do handyman work with Sam Torres," David said. He faced Delgado, an idea taking shape in his mind. "Why don't I paint your office for you? You'd be surprised at the difference a fresh coat of paint can make."

Delgado slowly ran his gaze over the boy, then nodded. "I guess that would be okay. You could finish it while I'm busy with this trial. I'm hardly ever here."

"I can start tomorrow after school," David said. "We have an early release day so I can move all the furniture to the middle of the room. I'll buy the paint and roll the walls the next day."

"Do you need help moving this stuff?" Delgado asked, pointing to the furniture scattered about the room.

David shook his head. "I can take care of all of it," he said. "No need to get anyone to help me."

"How much?"

"One fifty plus the cost of the paint."

"One thirty and you've got yourself a deal," Delgado said. "Just paint it the same color as it is now. And I want you done and outta here before the weekend," he said. "No dillydallying."

David nodded his agreement. The last thing he intended to do was delay. He wanted to have uninterrupted access to Delgado's office; he didn't care if he had to stay up all night to finish the job. If Delgado had that third spreadsheet, it must be in that filing cabinet. David would turn the office inside out until he found the key.

"Anything else?" Delgado asked, looking at him quizzically.

"No, sir. The next time you set foot in this office, it'll be gleaming with a fresh coat of paint."

Chapter 20

David took the stairs two at a time the next day. He had barely been able to sleep the night before. He hadn't even told Sam about his plan when he'd gone by Sam's house the prior evening to borrow tarps, brushes, and a paint tray.

It was shortly after noon and he knew Delgado was in trial. He barricaded the door with a chair as a precaution; he had to move all of the furniture in order to paint anyway. Locking the door would surely raise suspicions if anyone came upstairs to check on him.

David looked through every drawer in the desk, being careful not to disturb any of the contents. He didn't find the key to the filing cabinet. He made a meticulous search through the detritus and junk that filed the bookcase and thought he'd hit pay dirt when he found a small glass jar full of keys. None of them opened the filing cabinet.

He checked the time on his phone. He'd been there for almost two hours, and it didn't look like he'd accomplished anything. If the old man downstairs came to check on him, he'd be suspicious. David reluctantly abandoned his search for the key and began gathering the newspapers and used Styrofoam cups littering the office. He pushed against the desk but found it wouldn't budge.

David removed the top desk drawer and placed it on the floor. He again tried to slide the desk, to no avail. He removed the middle drawer and stacked it on top of the first drawer. This time, the desk moved. It took him another two hours to place all of the furniture and clutter in the messy office into the middle of the floor. He covered the newly created mound with the borrowed tarps and proceeded to tape off the ceiling, windows, and baseboards. He'd just finished when he heard a heavy tread on the stairs. David moved the chair barricading the door just as the old man knocked once and turned the knob, pushing the door open.

He stepped into the office and scanned the space. "You done a real good job, kid. This place was a pigsty. When you said you was gonna paint up here, I thought you were nuts."

David shrugged. "It took me longer than expected to get it ready. I'll be back tomorrow after school with the paint."

The man held the door for David and followed him out, locking the office. David would have to wait until the next day to continue searching for the filing cabinet key.

———

David paced while the man at the paint counter at Westbury Hardware discussed paint samples with an elderly woman. The woman looked over her shoulder at David and smiled. "This young man looks like he knows what he wants. Why don't you help him and let me think about this?"

"Thank you." David smiled at her and stepped to the counter. "Two gallons of interior white. Eggshell finish."

"What color, exactly?" the man asked.

"Doesn't matter. I'm just giving a fresh coat of paint to walls in an office."

The man led him to a row of cans along the wall. "These are all pre-mixed," he said.

David picked up two gallons and headed to the register. By the time he took the bus across town, it would be close to five o'clock. He figured it would take him at least two hours to roll the walls. The paint would dry fast and he'd be able to put most of the furniture back tonight, but he wouldn't have much time to look for the filing cabinet key.

He paid for the paint and ran to the bus stop to catch the four thirty bus.

———

David sprinted up the stairs to Delgado's office and worked as fast as he dared. Sam had taught him to move slowly and carefully, especially when painting. "Spills can be disastrous," Sam was fond of saying. "Doing it right the first time is always the most efficient way to work." Tonight, David ignored this advice and attacked the job with a vengeance. He was racing the clock.

He finished rolling the last wall and stepped back to view his work, looking for spots he might have missed. He didn't notice the paint tray in his path and stepped on one end of it, tilting it upward and splattering paint onto the floor. "What the …" he cried as he jumped back. He lunged for a rag and began sopping up the spilled paint. By the time he'd cleaned up his mess, he'd used every rag and paper towel he could find.

He cursed as he removed the tarp from the items in the middle of the room and began to reassemble the office. It'd taken him thirty precious minutes to clean up his mistake—time he wouldn't have to search for the key.

Moving faster than ever, he picked up the middle desk drawer and carried it to the desk. His foot caught in a torn spot on the carpet and the contents of the drawer spilled to the floor. David dropped the drawer at his feet in frustration and stopped short, his gaze fastened on the drawer. The bottom had sprung loose when it hit the floor.

David bent and removed the false bottom. Hidden underneath was a black notebook and a single silver key. David took the key to the filing cabinet. It fit the lock and he opened the top drawer. David let out a low whistle and began going through each file folder as quickly as possible. Most of them contained invoices and papers he recognized as relating to the liquor store business. The bottom drawer, however, held what he'd been certain he'd find: a slim file folder containing yellow legal pad pages bearing rows and rows of numbers in his father's neat hand.

David removed the file folder from the drawer and brought it to his chest. He stood, fighting the emotions welling up in him. He'd found what they needed to put Delgado away—he was certain of it. He took a deep breath and sprang into action.

He moved the copy machine back into its place on the corner of Delgado's desk and made a copy of the papers. David didn't notice the smudge of paint that had transferred from his shirt to the back of the file. He folded the copies, zipping them into the pocket of his jacket, and replaced the file in the bottom drawer of the cabinet. He pushed the lock shut and returned the key to the drawer. He was about to flip through the black notebook when he heard someone coming up the stairs.

David quickly replaced the false bottom of the drawer. He was pushing the drawer shut when the man opened the door.

"Look at this," the man said, scanning the room. "It's presentable in here, now." He faced David. "I know it's a school night. We're slow downstairs so I came up here to help you."

David was breathing hard. "You don't need to do that. I can finish up."

The man had already started moving a chair into place. "Nonsense. We'll be done in fifteen minutes, and you'll be on your way."

David nodded and wiped a paint-smeared hand across his brow. He glanced at his jacket; he had what he needed. The man gestured to him to help move the bookcase, and David obliged.

———

Chuck Delgado trudged up the stairs to his office. Sitting in that courtroom was like eight hours on the rock pile. He was exhausted. His attorney assured him the case was going well, but he wasn't so sure. The lawyer seemed more interested in his own publicity than in getting Delgado off for Delgado's sake. He was glad he had possession of that spreadsheet. He hadn't even told his lawyer about it. Some things were best kept secret. He could always disclose it later if he needed to.

Delgado inserted his key into the lock and was greeted with the aroma of fresh paint as he pushed the door open. He flipped on the overhead light and stood in the doorway, surveying the tidy room. It looked nice, he had to admit. He sat at his desk and surveyed his surroundings. The kid had done a good job.

He reached for his bottle of Jameson and poured himself a generous portion. He put his feet up on his tidy desktop, then quickly put them down. He drained his glass and poured another. The place was too neat, he decided. It was positively unnerving.

Delgado got to his feet and spread the papers across his desk that had been neatly stacked on the corner. He stood back and sighed. That was better. He spent the next thirty minutes restoring the chaos that was native to his office. When he came to the filing cabinet, he checked the lock and noted the smear of paint on one of the handles.

He stopped in his tracks. The cabinet had been locked; he was certain of it. That paint could have been deposited on the handle when they were moving the cabinet. He released the breath he'd been holding and returned to his desk, slumping into his chair. He reached again for his bottle of Jameson. He had it halfway to his glass when he dropped it heavily back onto his desk. He had to know that the spreadsheet was safe.

Delgado emptied the middle desk drawer, tossing the jumble of items onto his desk. He lifted the false bottom and retrieved the filing cabinet key. Delgado quickly went through each drawer. Nothing looked like it had been disturbed. He was about to lock up the cabinet when he stopped and pulled out the bottom drawer again. Holding that spreadsheet that William Wheeler had made—the one that would prove their case against him—always made him feel good.

He pulled the folder out of the cabinet and retraced his steps to his desk. He sat and paged slowly through the sheaves of legal pad paper bearing rows of numbers; many of which belonged to his own bank accounts. He smiled and poured himself another drink. His father had always told him he was the luckier of his two sons. "Here's to you, Dad." Delgado raised his glass in salute and took a large swallow.

He replaced the papers neatly in the folder and stood to return it to its locked drawer for safekeeping. As he turned the file over, he noticed the unmistakable smear of paint on the back. He matched the color to the newly painted walls.

Delgado froze, allowing his booze-fogged brain to process this new information. The folder contained four pages. He moved swiftly to the copy machine and noted the read out showing the total number of copies that had been made.

Every morning, he updated the record he kept in the top drawer of his desk of the number of copies that had been made on his machine. He didn't trust his employees—including that old man downstairs. He pulled out that record now and let out a low, guttural moan. Four copies had been made since that morning.

David Wheeler had had access to the room with plenty of time to search it. Delgado lowered his head into this hands. David Wheeler had motive, too. Plenty of it; the kid wanted to clear his father. How could he have been so stupid as to let Wheeler's kid have access to his office?

Delgado began to pace. He'd have to deal with this. He couldn't let the kid turn over what he had. And he couldn't trust anyone else to take care of this for him. It was too important. The only person he could trust was himself. He'd been content to leave Wheeler's family out of it. Hell—he'd even given this kid a job. And now the kid was making a fool out of Delgado.

Probably laughing his ass off somewhere. "We'll see about that," he muttered. "This won't seem funny when I'm after you and you have nowhere to hide."

Chapter 21

Frank Haynes looked up from his computer screen. Someone was rapping on the door to Haynes Enterprises with what sounded like a set of keys. He checked his watch. It was six thirty in the morning. Loretta didn't come in until later and she had her own key, anyway.

He rolled his chair over to the window overlooking the parking lot and opened the blinds a sliver. Chuck Delgado's monstrous Cadillac was pulled to the curb in the No Parking zone. Frank heaved himself from his chair and went to the door.

"What do you want?" he said through the glass. "You know we shouldn't be seen together. Your lawyer told you that."

"Open up, asshole," Delgado replied. "I've got somethin' to say to you. Somethin' you need to hear."

Frank reluctantly unlocked the deadbolt and stepped back as Delgado brushed past him, into the office.

Frank swept his gaze over the parking lot; theirs were the only two cars in sight.

"Make it fast. People start arriving for work by seven."

"You mean I might get to see that good lookin' assistant of yours, Frankie boy? We still have some unfinished business, she and I."

Frank spun on him, grabbed his arms, and slammed him into the wall. "You are done with Loretta, you hear me? Don't go near her; don't talk about her; don't even think about her."

Delgado smirked and tried to shake himself free.

Frank tightened his grip and leaned into Delgado. "I promise you this: if you hurt her or her kids, I won't rest until you pay for it."

"I've got the best lawyer in the country. You've seen that. The law isn't too good at making me pay."

"I'm not talking about the authorities getting to you. I've got friends in Miami, remember? And they'd make your friends in Chicago turn pale. You don't want to mess with me." He released one of Delgado's arms and shoved him toward the door.

"I didn't come here to talk about her. I don't give a shit about Loretta. There's a million broads like her. You can have her."

"Then why did you come?"

"I wanted to warn you about the Wheeler kid. The one you've taken under your wing with that dog of his. Seems he's poking his nose into our business, Frankie."

"What do you mean? David's a nice kid and doesn't have anything to do with this."

"That's where you're wrong. I hired him to paint my office, and he did some snooping—managed to find some papers that he shouldn't have."

"You don't know that."

Delgado looked into Frank's eye. "I do know that. And what he has will send both of us to jail."

Frank dropped his grip on Delgado's arm.

"I came by to see if you want to be part of the solution—what with all of your Miami connections."

"What do you mean 'solution'?" Haynes asked.

"The permanent kind. And soon. We can't let the kid take this stuff to Scanlon or Martin."

"I won't have any part of this," Frank said. "David Wheeler is innocent. You need to leave him alone, just like you need to leave Loretta alone. If anything happens to either one of them, I'll come after you."

"What David has will put you away, too, you idiot. Tell you what, get those papers from him and I'll leave him alone. But the minute I find out that he's contacted Scanlon or Martin—*kapow*," he said, pointing his index finger at Frank and bringing his thumb down to meet it. "I'll be watching him."

Both men turned as Loretta inserted her key in the lock and entered the office.

"I wanted to get an early start on—" Loretta stopped as she took in the scene in front of her.

"I was just leaving," Delgado said. He nodded to Frank and stepped to the door without glancing at Loretta. "Remember what I said, Frankie. This will be my only warning." He opened the door and made his exit.

Loretta spun on Frank.

Frank turned away.

She stepped to him and took his arm, turning him to face her. A line of perspiration sat on his upper lip.

"What in the world was that creep doing here?" she asked. "I thought you didn't have anything to do with him, now that he's not on the town council anymore."

Frank swallowed and tried to smile, but she could see fear in his eyes.

"I don't want you to be in this office anytime that I'm not here. No more coming in early or staying late."

"That's not very practical, Frank. I'll just keep the door locked."

Frank shook his head emphatically. "As long as he's on the loose, that's the way it's going to be."

"All right. But I don't want you to be near him, either."

"I'm fine. As I've said, you don't need to worry about me."

Loretta put her hand on his cheek. "He threatened you, Frank. I can see it in your eyes—you're afraid of him."

Frank brushed her hand aside. "I can take care of Delgado. You just take care of yourself and the kids." He stepped into his office and concentrated on shutting his door without slamming it shut.

He slumped into his chair and leaned over the desktop, cradling his head in his hands. He'd never intended for things to get this bad. Not only were the woman he loved and her children in danger, but Delgado was threatening the boy Frank had come to love like a son. Thank God, he still had that jump drive. If necessary, he could go to the police with it. The evidence on that drive would put Delgado away for decades, but it would also put Frank away. His hand shook as he reached for his coffee cup. If it came to that, would he possess the courage to do the right thing?

Chapter 22

Chuck Delgado turned down the volume on the talk radio channel as David Wheeler emerged from the deserted town square, his dog trotting at his side. He'd been watching the kid for the past week. If David kept to plan, he'd turn right at the end of the block and go home for the night. Maybe Frank Haynes had heeded his warning and had a talk with the boy.

Delgado shifted uncomfortably in his seat and turned up the heater. It'd been decades since he'd done surveillance work, and he didn't miss it. Still, he had to do this job himself.

David stopped at the edge of the square, waiting for the light to change so he could cross the street.

Delgado put his car into gear on the other side of the square and crept forward. He watched as the light changed and David crossed the street instead of turning right. The boy walked to the rear of Town Hall.

Delgado drove through the intersection and parked his car at the curb on the opposite side of the building. He walked quickly toward the rear of the building and cautiously peered around the corner.

Only three cars were in the parking lot at this late hour, and he recognized them all. They belonged to Maggie Martin, Alex Scanlon, and Frank Haynes. A dog began to whine, and he saw that the kid's dog was tied to Haynes' bumper and pulling on its leash. The back door of Town Hall opened, and David Wheeler crossed the parking lot, sprinted up the steps, and pulled papers out of his jacket pocket. Delgado froze.

He heard excited male voices exchange words that he couldn't distinguish. David stepped through the door, and it shut with a loud clang. That kid must be turning in the spreadsheet copies. Haynes hadn't scared the kid off. He'd deal with Haynes later. Right now, he had to take care of the kid and anyone with him.

Delgado snickered as he removed a Town Hall key from his pocket. Had they really thought he would turn over his copy of the key when they removed him from his town council seat? He made his way to the rear door and quietly let himself into the building. He entered the south stairwell and made his way to the top floor where the councilmembers' and mayor's offices were located.

He was breathing heavily when he reached his destination. Delgado removed his handkerchief and swiped it across his forehead and neck before easing the door open and entering the dark hallway. Keeping to the wall, he proceeded down the hall until he came to the mayor's suite. He gingerly tried the door and found it locked. No light shone from under the door.

Delgado resumed his search and made the turn at the end of the hallway. A pool of light spilled onto the carpet from an open door on his right. Frank Haynes' office. He crept slowly forward and stopped to listen. He heard a drawer being pulled open and shut, but no voices. Frank wasn't with the others.

Delgado carefully retraced his steps and re-entered the stairwell. He leaned heavily on the railing as he slowly descended. If they weren't upstairs, where were they? He'd seen David enter the building.

When he reached the first floor, he went to the rear door and verified that the three cars remained in the lot. He was shutting the door when the thought hit him. There was an old conference room in the basement. They'd used it as the council chambers years ago when the library occupied the top floor. When the do-gooders in town had finally raised enough money to build the new library, they'd remodeled the top floor into the executive offices and the council chambers. Scanlon must be using the basement space as his war room.

Delgado threw back his head to laugh, then slapped his hand over his mouth to muffle the sound. He had his two biggest enemies plus that nosey Wheeler kid trapped, and he knew what he was going to do with them.

———

Delgado quickly made his way to the basement. He had been part of the town council when they'd met downstairs. He still knew the layout like the back of his hand.

He opened the stairwell door slowly, listening for any sound. He knew he was on the far side of the building from the former council chambers. Delgado slipped into the dark hallway and paused, allowing his eyes to adjust to the low light. The large janitorial closet for the building was along this corridor. He inched toward it, keeping one hand on the wall and sliding one foot in front of him in case something obstructed his path.

Delgado found the closet unlocked and used the flashlight on his cell phone to survey the contents. He smiled broadly when he saw the gallon jug of hand sanitizer. He grabbed it with one hand and reached for a mop when he spotted a pipe in the corner better suited to his needs.

Using the heavy pipe as a guide, he edged his way back down the dark, narrow corridor that intersected with the wide hallway leading to the former council chambers. At the end of the carpeted hall, a crack of light outlined the double wooden doors of the room he was seeking. The Wheeler kid, Scanlon, and Martin had to be in there. And Haynes was on the top floor. His plan would take care of all of them.

Delgado slid the pipe through the heavy door handles and tilted it so that the end of the pipe was secured in the carpet, then opened the jug of hand sanitizer and began to pour. When the jug was empty, he reached into his pocket, withdrew his lighter, and set flame to the liquid. He watched, mesmerized, as the flames crawled a serpentine path toward the doors.

Delgado turned and retraced his steps, using his cell phone flashlight to speed his progress. He was pushing against the stairwell door when he noticed the sign on a door to his right marked "Electrical Panel."

He yanked open the door, shined his flashlight on the array of wires, and found the main circuit breaker switch.

Delgado rushed through the rear exit and drove off. If he made it to his office without anyone seeing him, he'd be home free.

Frank cursed under his breath when the lights in his office went out. They weren't in the middle of an electrical storm. There must have been an accident on the highway that took out a transformer. He fumbled in his desk drawer for his flashlight and swept the papers on his desk into his briefcase. He'd have to finish his work at home. He donned his coat, picked up his briefcase and flashlight, and made his way to the south stairwell.

He exited through the rear entrance and was surprised to find Dodger tied to his car, leaping about and barking frantically, straining at his leash. Frank ran to the familiar dog.

"What are you doing here, boy?" He bent to quiet the frantic animal. "Where's David?" He stood and cupped his hands around his mouth. "David?" he called at the top of his voice.

Frank ran from one end of the parking lot to the other, calling for David, as Dodger resumed barking. He noted that Alex's and Maggie's cars were in the lot. If they were in the building, why hadn't they made their way outside when the power went out?

He raced back up the steps to the rear entrance and smelled smoke as soon as he opened the door. He dialed 9-1-1 as he ran to the stairwell. As soon as he opened the door, he realized that the fire was in the basement.

Frank grabbed the hem of his coat and held it over his nose as he ran down the stairs. He saw the red glow from the wide hallway at the end of the corridor before he heard the cries for help. David must be in the old council chambers. David—and Maggie and Alex. Frank charged down the hall.

He made the turn onto the main corridor, the doors ahead of him fully engulfed in flame. He tasted bile when he saw that the door had been barricaded.

Frank removed his coat and used it to grasp the pipe and wrestle it free of the door handles. The flames caught his coat and he tossed it aside. "They're coming!" he screamed, hoping the three trapped in the room could hear him. He turned and retraced his steps, searching for a fire extinguisher. He found one twenty feet further down the hall and yanked it off the wall. Frank raced back to the double doors and began to spray the flames, but they were beyond his control. The fire extinguisher was almost empty when a set of large gloved hands grasped his shoulders and pulled him back.

Frank staggered. As he dropped the canister, he felt someone lift him onto their shoulder and carry him away. Salty tears stung his face as he tried to make them understand: David was in there. His David was in there.

Chapter 23

John Allen woke up on the couch to find the television airing a late-night talk show and Blossom, Buttercup, and Bubbles plastered along the length of his body. His wife, once again, was burning the midnight oil. He'd gotten used to having her around during their honeymoon, and he resented these all-too-frequent late evenings. He picked up his phone to call her and then set it back down. She was probably too busy to talk to him, anyway.

He gently dislodged the sleeping cats and whistled for the dogs. He'd take them outside for their last comfort break and head for bed. John had just turned out the light when the call came in. He'd assumed it would be Maggie, apologizing for not being home yet again. He was surprised when he saw the call was from Mercy Hospital.

"Dr. John Allen?" asked the official-sounding voice on the other end of the line.

John's blood ran cold. "Yes, that's me."

"I'm sorry to report that your wife and three others have just been brought in for treatment after a fire broke out at Town Hall."

John knew Maggie and Alex were spending their evenings in the basement—not where one would want to be when a fire broke out.

"Is she all right?"

"She's being seen by the doctors now. I'm sorry, but I don't have any other information to give you, sir. I suggest that you come down here."

"I'm on my way." John punched off the call, snatched his keys from his nightstand, and ran to his car. He ignored all speed limits on the way to the hospital, parked in the no-parking zone outside the emergency room, and tore through the double doors.

The nurse at the reception desk recognized him and took him to a quiet room. He paced, opening and closing his fists. He'd waited more than fifty years to meet the love of his life. He couldn't lose her now.

He turned as Marc Benson joined him. The two men faced each other in silence. Before they could speak, Jackie Wheeler was ushered into the room. She was crying, huge tears slipping unheeded down her cheeks. Marc pulled her to him, patting her on the back. William Wheeler's widow had been through a lot in these last few years and the strain showed in the creases on her forehead and the shadows under her eyes.

"I'm Alex Scanlon's partner, Marc," he said. "I don't think we've ever met."

She shook her head against his chest. "I just lost his father—I can't lose him," she sobbed.

"We don't have any reason to think that we're going to lose anyone," John said. "I know it's hard, but we need to wait to hear what the doctors have to say."

"What was he doing with Maggie and Alex?" Jackie pulled her head back and looked at John. "I thought he was out walking his dog, like he does every night. Why was he at Town Hall?"

John shook his head.

The distraught family members turned at the knock on the door. Three doctors entered the room. "We'll need to meet with each of you individually to discuss the specifics of your family members' injuries, but I can tell you that they're all going to be fine. We're keeping them overnight for observation but expect them all to be released in the morning."

Jackie Wheeler put her hand to her heart, and Marc rocked back on his heels.

"Then everyone got out safely," John said.

"Not exactly," one of the doctors replied. "Another person was in the building and came to their rescue. The doctors are with him now. His injuries may be significant."

"Can you tell us who saved them?" John asked.

"Frank Haynes," said the doctor. "Councilman Frank Haynes."

———

Maggie woke shortly before six the next morning and turned to find John dozing in a chair at her bedside. She reached for his hand, and he opened his eyes.

"You're looking better this morning," he said. "How are you feeling?"

"Physically, I'm fine. Mentally, I'm a mess. I can't begin to tell you how terrifying that was."

John moved her tray table aside and sat on the edge of the bed. "It's incomprehensible. I don't know what to say." He rubbed her arm and looked away.

Maggie looked at her husband. "This must have been traumatic for you, too. Did you sleep last night?"

John shrugged.

"The doctor's going to recommend a therapist," she said. "You should come with me."

"Maybe I will."

"Has Chief Thomas talked to you? Do they have any idea what happened?"

"They've confirmed that it was arson. They assume Delgado or one of his goons. They're on the scene with the fire marshal, gathering evidence. They don't have anything yet."

Maggie's voice caught in her throat. "They've got to get this guy."

John's tone was full of steel. "They will. Chief Thomas said the feds will be involved now."

"What about the others?" Maggie asked.

"David and Alex are doing well."

"There's something else I need to tell you." John drew a deep breath. "Frank was the one who saved you. He reported the fire and went into the basement and removed a metal pipe that was barricading the door. That's why they're so sure it was intentionally set."

Maggie looked past John, focusing on the wall behind him. "I knew someone was calling to us. I thought it was the firefighters. I thought the fire alarm went off."

John took her hands in his. "It didn't. The electrical power was disabled at the main switch. Frank was working late and left the building when the lights went out. He saw your cars in the lot and came back inside to search for you. He smelled the fire."

Maggie stared.

"He fought through the smoke and fire in the basement to find the door barred. He sustained serious burns removing the metal pipe that had you barricaded." He reached a hand to touch her cheek. "The firefighters arrived in the nick of time. All four of you could have been killed."

"How is Frank?"

"He's in stable condition. He'll be in the burn unit for a while. He was able to talk to the police, but they now have him heavily sedated."

"Did he see anyone or anything suspicious?"

John shook his head.

Maggie leaned forward. "You need to go to Loretta. Someone has to tell her about Frank."

"The police will stop by Haynes Enterprises this morning," he said.

"She shouldn't hear it from the police, John. She has feelings for Frank." Maggie fixed him with her gaze. "You know that's true. You saw it at the hospital when Nicole and Susan were undergoing surgery."

John brought her hand to his lips and kissed it. "After everything this woman's done to you, you're concerned about her feelings?"

Maggie nodded. "Loretta never intended to hurt me, John. She fell for Paul and believed all the lies he told her. She wouldn't be the first woman to fall victim to his charms—he had me fooled for years. The truth is, we've formed a bond, Loretta and I. If I were up to it, I'd tell her myself. This can't wait. I want you to go to her now."

———

John was walking across the hospital parking lot when he heard someone call his name. He turned to find Sam and Joan Torres hurrying toward him.

"How are they?" Sam called as they approached.

"Maggie, Alex, and David are all doing well."

"David!" Sam cried. "What was David doing there?"

John shrugged. "I don't know."

"Thank God, they're okay," Joan said, letting out a deep breath. "I prayed all the way over here."

"How did you hear?" John asked.

"It was on the local news," Sam said. "They named Maggie and Alex and said that there were two others. Who's the fourth person?"

"Frank Haynes," John supplied.

"The news said one of them was in stable but serious condition. That must be Frank?"

John nodded. "What information did you get from the news report?"

"Just that there was a fire that started in the basement of Town Hall and the origin of the fire is under investigation." Sam stared at John. "They suspect arson again, don't they?"

"This isn't for public knowledge, but they won't be able to keep it quiet for long. Yes. Another arson."

Joan gasped. "Why would anyone want to destroy Town Hall?"

Sam turned to his wife. "That may not have been their goal." He turned back to John. "Was someone trying to kill all four of them?"

John shook his head. "Only Maggie, Alex, and David were in that basement. Frank was working upstairs and risked his life to save them."

Sam rocked back on his heels and let out a low whistle. "Will wonders never cease."

"And he's the most seriously injured?" Joan asked.

John nodded.

"Who's up there with them?" Joan straightened her spine, and John recognized a woman who was about to take charge.

"Jackie is with David, and Marc is with Alex. I stayed with Maggie, but she's sent me out to tell Loretta. Frank is all alone."

"Not anymore, he's not," Joan declared, reaching into her purse for her cell phone. "We're going to take care of Frank Haynes."

Chapter 24

John paced outside Haynes Enterprises, rehearsing what he would say to Loretta. His was the only car in the lot. He looked at his watch; it was shortly after seven. He hoped she hadn't seen the news reports about the fire. Maggie was right—Loretta deserved to hear about it in person.

A car turned into the lot, and he recognized Loretta behind the wheel. She pulled into a parking spot and looked at him quizzically as she approached the entrance.

John nodded to her. "Good morning," he called.

"What are you doing here?"

John stood in front of her and took a deep breath. "Did you hear about the fire at Town Hall last night?"

The color drained from Loretta's face as she shook her head. "I don't have time to read the paper in the morning, and I didn't have the news on. I was too busy getting the kids ready for school."

"Let's go inside," John said, taking her arm.

Loretta wrenched it free. "No. Something's happened. Tell me now." Her voice rose to a high pitch. "Is Frank okay?"

"He's in stable condition," John said. "He was at Town Hall last night when a fire broke out. He saved Maggie, Alex, and David Wheeler. If he hadn't acted when he did, they'd be dead."

Loretta swayed, and John reached out to steady her. "So he's going to be all right?"

John nodded. "They think so, yes. He's in the burn unit and heavily sedated—for the pain. But he was lucid enough to talk to the police earlier."

"The police? Why the police?"

"The fire was deliberately set. Someone barricaded Maggie, Alex, and David in a room in the basement and set the fire. They were trying to kill them."

"Delgado," Loretta exclaimed. "It has to be Delgado."

"They don't know who did it. Yet."

Loretta leaned over and put her head in her hands, then threw them back as she stood. "How are the others, John? Is Maggie all right?"

"Thanks to Frank," John said, "they're all fine. They kept them in the hospital overnight, but they're going to be released today."

Loretta took a deep breath. "That's good. I'm glad." She raised her eyes to his. "I need to go to him."

"You're in no condition to drive. I'll take you."

"I might want to stay there all day," Loretta protested. "You said he's sedated. I want to make sure he knows I'm there."

"I'll make arrangements to get your car to the hospital." He put his hand on her back and steered her to his car. "For now, you're coming with me."

John looked for a parking space, navigating the Mercy Hospital lot that had become a labyrinth of news vans, reporters, and cameras. It looked like the Town of Westbury would be making national news once again.

"Why don't I let you off here?" he said, pulling up to the entrance. "You go on ahead, and I'll park the car and come find you."

Loretta shook her head in vehement denial. "I don't want to go through all of those people on my own. You need to come with me."

John pursed his lips and was about to object when someone tapped on the driver's side window. He and Loretta both turned their attention from the hospital entrance to find George Holmes motioning for John to open the window. Tonya was at George's side.

"We just heard. I parked four blocks over on a residential street," George said. "You won't find a spot in the lot."

"I was trying to convince Loretta to let me drop her off," John said.

"I'm not sure I can get through that crowd," Loretta said, holding back tears.

"George will get you through. Don't you worry about a thing," Tonya said, bending down to smile at Loretta.

Tonya's husband came around to the passenger side and opened the door for Loretta. He offered her his hand, and she reluctantly stepped out of the car. Next to his six-foot-six muscular frame, Loretta looked like a paper doll. He put his arm around her shoulder protectively and gently urged her forward.

John watched the sea of people part as George, Loretta, and Tonya made their way to the lobby, turned in the direction of the elevators, and disappeared from view.

―⁂―

Loretta hesitated at the door to the hospital waiting room. It was packed with all of Maggie's friends. She was about to turn around and find another place to wait when Gloria Vaughn noticed her standing in the doorway. The old woman rose stiffly to her feet and beckoned to Loretta to come in.

"We've been waiting for you, dear," she said as Judy Young rose from the chair next to Gloria and motioned for her to sit down in her place.

"Do you know me?" Loretta asked.

"I've seen you in Celebrations," Judy replied. "That's my shop."

"We know that you're Nicole's mother and that you are a special person in Frank's life," Gloria said.

Loretta felt tears prick the back of her eyes.

Gloria placed her hand over Loretta's. "This must be a horrible shock for you."

Loretta nodded, making no move to remove her hand from under Gloria's.

"It's been a shock for all of us," Gloria said.

"Are you here for Maggie?"

Judy knelt next to Loretta. "Maggie, Alex, and David are doing well, and we've heard they'll be discharged today or tomorrow." She held Loretta's gaze. "We're here for Frank. And for you, Loretta."

Loretta could no longer restrain her tears, and they slid silently down her face.

"You'll get through this," Gloria said softly. "You'll see. Don't let your mind race to scary places."

Loretta sniffed and nodded.

"You probably know that better than any of us," Judy said, handing her a tissue from her purse.

Loretta turned as a nurse stepped into the doorway and called her name.

"You can see Mr. Haynes now. Just for a few minutes," she said, motioning to Loretta to follow her.

Loretta squeezed Gloria's hand, then followed the nurse.

"Is he awake?" she asked.

The woman nodded. "He's come around and his vital signs are good."

"Is he going to survive?"

The nurse looked at her. "Yes. He had a good night. We think he's going to be fine." She stopped at a doorway and handed Loretta a hospital gown and gloves. "Put these on as a precaution. You'll dispose of them in this bin when you leave," she said, pointing to a receptacle inside the door.

"Mr. Haynes," the nurse said as Loretta hastily washed her hands and donned the gown and gloves. "I've got someone to see you."

Frank Haynes lay flat on his back, a breathing apparatus over his mouth. He was hooked up to a handful of machines that blinked and beeped behind his bed. He turned his head and Loretta could see by his eyes that he was smiling.

She stepped to the side of his bed and grasped the railing with both hands. "Oh, Frank," she said and choked on the words.

He shook his head imperceptibly.

Loretta drew a deep breath to steady herself. "I hear you were a hero. That you saved Maggie, Alex, and David from dying in the fire."

Frank raised an eyebrow.

"I'm proud of you, Frank. John met me at the office today to give me the news and bring me here." Loretta leaned closer to him. "That was very brave of you. The waiting room is full of people concerned about you, Frank."

He furrowed his brow as if he couldn't take in what she was saying to him.

"Seriously, Frank. The waiting room is packed, and Gloria Vaughn told me they're all here for you."

Frank reached for his oxygen mask with a bandaged hand and pulled it away from his mouth. "They're here for the others." he rasped.

"Nope. The others are going to be discharged today or tomorrow. They're alive, thanks to you. And the nurse told me that you're doing well, too." Loretta smiled down at him.

Frank nodded.

"This was Delgado's doing, wasn't it, Frank? He was trying to kill all three of them. He almost succeeded—and he almost killed you, too."

Frank pulled the mask from his face again. "Take money from me and buy plane tickets for you and the kids. Get out of Westbury until this is over."

"And leave you here, like this? Not a chance."

"Go," Frank said as forcefully as he could. "I can stop Delgado."

Loretta looked at the man she loved. *I can stop Delgado, too,* she thought. It was time to go to the authorities with the copy of the jump drive that she'd taken from Frank's safe. She was more certain than ever that it contained the evidence necessary to convict Delgado. She also feared that it contained information that would incriminate Frank. If she turned it in— turned Frank in—he'd never forgive her. But if she didn't, Delgado might never get locked up. She couldn't allow Delgado to remain a menace to the people she loved.

"No matter what happens, Frank, remember, I love you."

Chapter 25

Aaron Scanlon placed his phone on the kitchen counter and went in search of his wife. He found Susan in their bedroom, struggling to pull her suitcase from the top shelf of their closet.

She turned as he stepped behind her and reached up to take the suitcase from her.

"We've got to go," she said. "We can't just stay here while someone is trying to murder my mother and your brother."

Aaron set the suitcase on the floor and took her in his arms. "My first reaction was to jump on a plane and get out there, too." He leaned back and put his hand under her chin, raising her face to his. "But be realistic— there's nothing we can do to help."

"I don't care," Susan pushed her hands against his chest. "I want to be there. I need to take care of my mother. Plus, the Easter carnival is a few weeks away, and she shouldn't have to do that alone."

"Alex told me she's fine." He looked into her eyes. "Did she ask you to come?"

Susan turned her head aside. "No," she mumbled. "But don't you want to go check on Alex?"

Aaron sighed heavily. "Like I said, there's nothing we can do, and the last thing they need are two more people underfoot right now."

"Is that what Alex told you?"

Aaron nodded. "Besides, you still haven't recovered. Donating a kidney to Nicole took a toll on you. You're just starting to regain your strength and stamina. Or you were. You seem to have a touch of the flu right now, and I want you to take care of yourself."

Susan arched an eyebrow at him.

"I heard you gagging in the bathroom right before your mother called. Are you feeling all right?" He slid his hand to her forehead.

She brushed it aside and sat on the edge of the bed. "I've had waves of nausea the last few days. I was going to tell you, but all this news of arson and attempted murder pushed it out of my mind."

"You don't want to get on a plane to fly across country right now," Aaron said. "And that's my medical opinion, as a doctor. Plus, they don't need us. Let's plan a trip for later this spring."

Susan slumped back onto the bed. "I suppose you're right. I'm exhausted and I don't feel that great."

Aaron drew the covers aside. "Get in and take a nap. When you wake up, I'll take you anywhere you want to go for dinner."

Susan took his hand and kissed it. "You're working out to be a really good husband. You've got a deal."

Frank Haynes lifted the cover from the luncheon tray the hospital staff had delivered while he dozed. The gelatinous glob of meat surrounded by mashed potatoes and mixed vegetables would have been barely palatable while it was warm; now that it was cold, it held no appeal whatsoever. He replaced the cover and opened the packet of saltines on the tray. As he nibbled the crackers, he realized he was ravenously hungry.

Someone knocked softly on his door, and Frank called, "Come in." If it were the nurse, he'd ask for another tray. He was surprised when Tonya Holmes and Tim Knudsen entered his room.

"Hey, Frank," Tonya said, a slow smile spreading across her face.

"How are you today?" Tim asked.

"I'm coming around," Frank replied. "Turns out, I wasn't hurt as badly as they first thought."

"We're all so relieved to hear that," Tonya said.

The three councilmembers stared at each other.

Tim broke the awkward silence. "That was an extremely brave thing you did, Frank. Not many people would have had the courage. You saved their lives."

Frank raised his hand to wave off their praise.

"Tim's right, Frank. You're a hero and we're all grateful."

Frank cleared his throat and looked aside. "Thank you."

Tonya looked at his tray table. "Have you eaten?"

Frank shook his head. "No. This is inedible." He pointed to the tray.

"Hungry?" Tim asked.

"Starving, actually."

"Good," Tonya held up a paper sack stamped with the logo of Pete's Bistro. "We brought you lunch from Pete's. It's a double-cut pork chop with Chinese char sui sauce, au gratin potatoes, and a slice of Dutch apple pie. Pete said it's your favorite."

Frank stared, mouth agape, as Tim removed the hospital tray and Tonya set out the meal she'd brought.

"This is awfully nice of you," Frank said. "What do I owe you?"

"This is on Pete," Tonya replied. "He called this morning to see if one of us was coming to see you. And he said he'll be sending dinner over every day until you're released. Gloria Vaughn and I already have you on a meal donation schedule when you get home."

"People will bring me meals at home?"

"You'd better believe it," Tonya replied. "We used an online website where people can login and sign up. The *Westbury Gazette* ran an article about it. So many people signed up that you'll have meals for at least three months."

Frank flushed. "I had no idea. I don't even know that many people." His voice cracked with emotion.

"We take care of our own in Westbury," Tonya said. "You know that. More people care about you than you realize, Frank." She slid the bedside table closer to him. "Now pick up your fork and start eating, or I might just help myself. That smells delicious."

Chapter 26

Maggie leapt out of her hospital bed as the door to her room began to open. "Did you bring my jacket?" she asked as she picked up the remote and turned off the television.

"I brought more than that," John replied, as Maggie's son and daughter-in-law stepped into the room ahead of him.

Maggie gasped. "What in the world? I thought the two of you were in Maui?"

"We were," Mike Martin replied. "And when we saw the news story, we decided to swing by here to see you on our way home."

"Westbury is a thousand miles away from being 'on the way home' from Hawaii to Southern California."

"We wanted to come see you, make sure you were all right," Amy said, leaning in to hug her mother-in-law. "It was my idea. I insisted."

Maggie took Amy's face in her hands. "Your trip was supposed to be a romantic getaway for the two of you. I hope you didn't cut it short to come see me."

Amy shook her head. "We extended our trip by one day. We have to go back home in the morning."

"Our timing seems perfect," Mike said. "We can help get you home and spend a quiet night at Rosemont." He encircled Amy in his arms. "It'll be the perfect way to end our vacation."

Maggie leaned back and looked at the couple who were so dear to her. They'd had a hard time after Amy's miscarriage. Amy had thrown herself into activities involving their twin daughters, Sophie and Sarah, and volunteered for every fundraiser, carpool, and school project. They'd overcommitted their schedules and spent little time together as a couple. Grief was taking its toll.

Amy squeezed Mike's hand, and he kissed the top of her head.

Maggie smiled. The week in Maui had been good for them. She turned to John. She'd been preoccupied with her duties as mayor and the case against Delgado—and now this. John had been shaken by the call from the hospital. She and John needed a romantic evening, too. As soon as Mike and Amy left to return to California, she knew where she'd take John.

"Let's get out of here and back to Rosemont. I think we should all get into our pajamas, order takeout, and watch romantic comedies."

———

"Are you sure you're up to going out to eat?" John asked as he turned his Suburban onto the winding road leading to The Mill.

"Positive," Maggie replied. "After watching all those movies yesterday, I'm in the mood for a romantic dinner."

John chuckled. "I think the romantic movies got to Mike and Amy, too. Did you see them at breakfast? Neither of them could keep their eyes open. At least they can sleep on the plane back to California."

"That's exactly what I'd hoped for," Maggie said. She shifted in her seat to face him. "They seemed happy together, didn't they?"

"Indeed they did."

Maggie sighed. "When I went to sleep last night, I said a prayer that they would have another child."

"Maybe even conceive it at Rosemont?" John glanced at her.

Maggie grinned sheepishly. "The thought did cross my mind ..."

"I think you may get your wish. When I dropped them at the airport this morning, Mike made a cryptic remark that he thought Rosemont might be a good luck charm. Something like that."

"Rosemont has certainly been that for me," Maggie said, squeezing his hand. "If I hadn't come to Rosemont and Eve hadn't been whimpering in the snow outside the library door, I'd never have met you."

John swung into the parking lot at The Mill. "The stars did align in our favor, didn't they? I never thought, after all of those years alone, that I would find the love of my life."

Maggie brushed a gloved hand across her eyes. "We're blessed, for sure." She leaned over and kissed John, long and deep. "That's why I wanted to come out here. I wanted to relive our first date."

John tucked a strand of hair behind her ear. "I'm glad it was so memorable. I hadn't planned anything romantic for years and wasn't sure I still knew how." He sighed. "It's too bad that they've closed the ice rink down. I don't think you're in any shape to skate, but it would be fun to watch people on the ice."

"About that," Maggie's eyes shown. "I took a leaf out of your book and talked them into keeping it open one last night—just for us. And I most certainly am 'in shape.' No excuses, Dr. Allen. After dinner, you are sashaying your wife around the ice."

Chapter 27

Sam Torres was stepping off the curb at the entrance to Mercy Hospital as a pretty blond teenage girl approached with a familiar one-eyed dog at the end of a leash. She was accompanied by a younger boy wearing huge glasses. Sam stopped and dropped to one knee. The usually well-mannered dog strained at the leash to greet him.

"Hello, Dodger," Sam said, rubbing the dog's ears as Dodger pranced happily in front of him. "I'm Sam Torres," he said, extending his hand to the girl.

"David works with you part time, doesn't he?" the girl said. "I'm Grace Acosta, and this is my brother, Tommy. We're friends of David's."

Sam nodded. "He's told me about you."

The girl smiled. "We thought it would cheer him up to have a visit from Dodger. Mrs. Wheeler let us bring him by."

"That's a grand idea," Sam said. "I just left him, and he's a bit down in the dumps."

Grace looked up sharply.

"The doctors want to keep him for an extra day. He's doing fine, but that's protocol for someone his age."

"Then I'm doubly glad we came," Grace said.

Tommy began pulling at her sleeve.

"I'll let the two of you get on," Sam said. "He'll enjoy your visit."

"What?" Grace snapped at her brother as he continued to pull her sleeve. He motioned for her to bend down to him. She obliged and he cupped her ear with his hand and whispered. When she stood, she was beaming. "Brilliant plan, Tommy. Let's make this happen.

The nurse behind the desk on the pediatrics floor grinned at the familiar dog. "I didn't think we'd see you for a while," she said to Dodger, stepping from behind her workstation to greet him. "What with David being in the hospital and all."

"That's why we're here," Grace said. "We came to bring Dodger to see David. We're not trained therapy dog handlers," she said, pointing to herself and her brother. "But we did want to see the kids before we went to David's room."

The nurse stood and looked at her quizzically.

"David has to stay until tomorrow, so we thought the kids here on the floor could make him a card or something."

"That's a wonderful idea," the nurse said. "There are a bunch of kids in the playroom. You go see David, and I'll get them started on it and bring the card up on my break." She checked her watch. "That'll be in twenty minutes."

Grace gestured to her brother. "All his idea."

The nurse looked at him thoughtfully. "You were in here a few months ago, weren't you? For eye surgery?"

Tommy nodded.

"Then you know firsthand how hard it is to be in the hospital. You're a very thoughtful young man," she said, patting Tommy on the arm.

Grace, Tommy, and Dodger walked back to the elevator as the nurse headed to the playroom.

———

David tossed the remote on the bed and turned to the door. "Yeah," he said, unable to keep the annoyance out of his voice.

"Hi, David," Tommy said. Grace had given him Dodger's leash, and the dog pulled him into the room.

"Dodger!" David cried, sitting up quickly. Dodger trotted to where David was now sitting up in bed. He paced along the side of the bed, wagging his tail furiously and looking longingly at his master.

David patted the mattress, and Dodger needed no further invitation. He launched himself onto the bed, and David embraced his dog. Dodger responded by covering his face with kisses.

Grace hung back.

David looked up at her and his expression melted her heart. "Was this your idea?" he asked.

Grace shook her head slowly and pointed to Tommy.

"This is the nicest thing anybody's ever done for me," David said, turning to Tommy. "Thanks, man," he said, extending his hand for a fist bump.

"I thought you'd like to see him. Dodger helped me a lot when I was in here."

"You're all the talk at school, you know," Grace said.

David shook his head. "That's the last thing I need."

"Everyone's saying you're a hero."

"I'm not, but Frank Haynes is."

"Well ..." Grace began and was interrupted by a knock on the door. The pediatric nurse came into the room, carrying an armload of colorful drawings.

"David," the nurse said. "The kids on pediatrics miss you and want you to know they're thinking of you and wish you well." She set the stack of papers on his tray table.

David picked up one of the drawings and flushed. It showed a stick figure of a man and a dog, and the man was wearing a Superman cape.

"See," Grace said, smiling. "Everyone thinks that you were brave to be at Town Hall that night."

David buried his face in Dodger's neck.

"You get better, David," the nurse said. "We can't wait until the two of you can visit us again."

"We'll be back," David said as Dodger stretched out next to him on the bed and settled his muzzle on his paws. "I'm supposed to go home tomorrow."

The nurse nodded to all three of them and left the room.

"That's good news," Grace said. "I've missed you at school."

"I thought you'd have a million other friends by now."

"Not really," Grace stepped to the bed and began to stroke Dodger. "Will you be able to come to the musical?"

"That's right," David said. "You're Cinderella, aren't you?"

"You remembered?" Grace brightened.

"Of course I did. I've already got my ticket for Friday night. That's when it starts, right?"

"Yes. That's opening night." Grace stopped stroking Dodger and smiled at David. "Since you're going to be there Friday night anyway, I was wondering if you'd like to come to the cast party with me afterward?"

David flushed. "Sure. That would be great."

Tommy pushed himself out of the chair where he'd been watching the two of them. "Geez, are you two done yet?"

David turned to the boy. "How's Magellan doing?"

"He's the greatest cat ever. He's so smart, and he knows exactly when I get home from school. He's waiting for me every day."

"Sounds like Namor," David said.

"Mags is a great hunter and explorer, too. He's already caught a mouse in the basement and brought it upstairs. My mom wasn't too happy about that."

David laughed. "My mom wouldn't be, either."

Dodger's ears perked up and he rose to a sitting position, then quickly jumped from the bed.

"I think that's the dinner cart," David said, grabbing for the leash and missing it. "Dodger!" he yelled as the dog darted out the door.

Tommy tore after him and caught the leash just as Dodger turned in the direction of the cart. He pulled Dodger back into David's room.

"Someone's going to need some refresher training before we come back here," David said sternly to his dog.

Dodger looked from Tommy to David and wagged his tail.

"You'd better get him out of here before he gets us all into trouble," David said.

Grace smiled at David. She took the leash from Tommy and brought Dodger to David's bed. "Say goodbye, Dodger. You'll see him tomorrow."

David leaned over and rubbed Dodger's ears. "Goodbye, boy. And be good. Don't get into any trouble on the way out of here, or we'll never be able to come back."

"I've got a good hold on his leash. He'll be fine," Grace said. "I'll see you when you get back to school."

"Thank you both for coming to see me and bringing Dodger." David held her gaze. "I appreciate it more than you know."

Chapter 28

Maggie and Alex made their way up the walkway to the front door of the former administration building at Highpointe College. Alex looked at the ornate brickwork on the facade. "Beautiful old building. It's nice of the college to let the town rent it out while Town Hall is being restored."

"I think they're glad to have the revenue," Maggie said. "The president told me that the building is on the national register of historic places, so they're not going to tear it down, but the process of getting approval for renovations is taking forever."

The police officer stationed at the door held it open for them.

"Amazing how quickly they got the phone lines installed." Alex scanned the busy lobby. A line of people waited to enter an adjacent room identified by a large handwritten sign taped to the wall that read "Clerk's Office." "Looks like Westbury is back in business."

They started across the space and a woman began to clap, followed by another and another, until the walls reverberated with the sound. Maggie flushed as Alex ushered her to a spot in the middle of the room and then stepped back.

Maggie raised her hands to silence the crowd. "Good morning. Alex and I want to thank you for that warm welcome. We're glad to be here this morning and grateful to the college for welcoming the town with open arms. As you know, you can't keep the good people of Westbury down. Police Chief Thomas is working diligently with the fire marshal to find out who set fire to Town Hall. In the meantime, construction to restore Town Hall is already underway. And now, Alex and I are going back to work." She turned to Alex.

"They were trying to kill you two and William Wheeler's son, weren't they?" called a man in the crowd.

Alex took Maggie's elbow and leaned close to her. "Don't take any questions. Let's get out of here."

Maggie nodded to Alex, and they continued to the stairway at the end of the lobby and mounted the steps to the office on the second floor designated to the mayor.

"Too bad there isn't a back way out of here," Maggie remarked as they hung their coats on a series of hooks inside the door.

"Adopt a policy of never talking to the press or giving statements when you come and go. If you don't, the press will camp out here and you'll never have a moment's peace. In fact, I'd find another venue altogether to hold press conferences," Alex advised.

"Good idea," Maggie said, pulling out the chair behind the large wooden desk that filled a quarter of the room. Alex drew up a chair opposite her and sat. They stared at each other in silence.

"Now what?" Maggie asked.

Alex shook his head. "I wish I knew. We have copies of everything in that room, backed up off site. Everything except that third spreadsheet that David brought us."

"And he didn't make a copy," Maggie supplied in a monotone. "I know we didn't have much time to look at it before the fire broke out, but what did you think?"

"It was the missing link we needed." Alex leaned forward and put his head in his hands. "We could've nailed Degaldo with it."

"And now?"

"Now we're right back where we were before. With an incomplete case against the bastard, that his lawyer can drive a truck through." Alex looked at Maggie and the pain behind his eyes was unmistakable. "He's going to walk away from all charges. And you, David, and I will spend the rest of our lives looking over our shoulders."

"I agree that Delgado tried to kill us." Maggie shuddered. "He's not a smart guy, and his luck has to run out sometime. Maybe he didn't cover his tracks with the fire, and they'll get him on that."

"Arson seems to be his specialty, remember?" Alex said, referring to the fires that destroyed his home and law office several years earlier. "He got away with those."

Maggie sighed heavily. "The feds are involved this time. Since the fire was attempted murder, rather than just the destruction of property, they're all over it. I have to think that this time will be different. Something's going to give here; we're going to get a lucky break. I can sense it."

Alex stood suddenly, tipping his chair back and sending it to the floor with a resounding *thwack*. "Stop with the pie-in-the-sky optimism, Maggie! I know it's your nature, but I'm sick of it. Time to face reality." He began to pace. "Aaron tells me that Susan has been pleading with you to get out of Westbury, sell Rosemont and move back to California? I'm starting to think you should consider it."

Maggie rose and walked around to the front of her desk. She stared at Alex until he stopped pacing. "John and I have discussed this," she said. "We are not leaving Westbury. Turning tail and running is not my style. We're going to put that weasel Delgado behind bars and make Westbury safe again. We're going to find the stolen pension money and restore it to the people who worked so hard to earn it."

Alex nodded slowly.

"You and Marc aren't leaving here, are you?"

"No," Alex admitted.

"Then let's not discuss this again. We've both got a lot of work to do to get this town back on track. Let's get started."

Maggie stretched and leaned toward her computer screen, noting the time displayed in the lower right corner. It was almost one thirty in the afternoon and she was ravenously hungry. Highpointe College had been nice enough to allow the town employees to buy meal tickets while Town Hall was housed in its temporary quarters on the college campus. The college cafeteria closed at two. She retrieved her coat from the hook by the door and struck out across campus.

The sun shone brightly in a cloudless sky, turning the late March snow into a glittering blanket. Maggie nodded at the students she passed, bundled in down jackets with backpacks laden with books slung across their shoulders.

The food service line was short and the attendants had already begun to remove the day's offerings from the steam tables. Maggie accepted a serving of shepherd's pie, something she remembered from her own college days. She'd never liked shepherd's pie and made a mental note to make her way to the cafeteria earlier the next time she planned to eat there.

She surveyed the scene in front of her, tray in hand. She began searching for an open seat when someone touched her elbow. She turned and recognized one of the students who had stayed to ask questions after her panel presentation.

"Mayor Martin," he said, "would you like to join us?"

"Thank you," Maggie said. "This place is packed."

"You're always welcome to sit with us," he said, leading her to a spot in the corner where a group of students had pushed two tables together. "We've sort of commandeered this corner. We're here every day."

A young woman slid her books to one side to make room for Maggie's tray while another young man procured a chair from another table.

"Did you have other questions for me?" Maggie asked as she sat.

"No," the boy said. "I just saw you standing there and ... well ..." he paused, collecting his thoughts, "we all like you. We think you're cool."

Maggie stopped with her fork halfway to her mouth. These kids thought she was cool? Would wonders never cease? Wait until she told John. "That's awfully nice of you," she managed to say.

The students returned to what seemed to be a heated discussion about the study of classical literature in the modern world. Maggie listened with a growing sense of contentment as she ate. *What a change from the pragmatic issues I deal with every day,* she thought. The ivory tower of academia sometimes seemed very attractive.

Chapter 29

Loretta left Haynes Enterprises shortly after one and walked purposefully to her car. She unzipped the interior pouch in her purse and verified, for what seemed like the hundredth time, that the copy of the jump drive was safely tucked inside. She'd heard on the news that Town Hall had taken up temporary headquarters at Highpointe College. She planned to drive directly there and surrender the jump drive to Alex.

She slid behind the wheel and paused before starting the ignition, staring into the distance. The jump drive almost certainly contained evidence that would incriminate Frank. By turning it over to Alex, she would be the catalyst for his arrest and possible imprisonment. The happy future she'd dreamed of for herself and her children would be gone. But if she didn't turn it in and others—including Frank—were hurt or killed, she'd never forgive herself. Even if it cost her the man she loved, she knew she was doing the right thing.

Her cell phone rang, startling her out of her reverie. She snatched the thing from her purse and saw that the call was from Frank. She debated letting it go to voice mail but decided against it and answered the call.

"Loretta," Frank said. "I'm so glad I got you. I need you to close the office and come here."

"I've just stepped out to run an errand. I planned to see you later this afternoon."

"I need you to come now, Loretta. Whatever you were going to do can wait." Something in his voice scared her.

"All right, Frank. I'm on my way." Loretta reluctantly turned her car in the direction of Mercy Hospital. She'd take care of whatever Frank needed and then head to Town Hall. She wouldn't tell him that she'd copied the jump drive. He'd eventually find out about her betrayal, and he'd despise her for it. But he didn't need to find out about it today while he was still recovering.

Loretta sat in the hospital parking lot, gathering her courage. She checked her hair and touched-up her lipstick in the rearview mirror, then forced herself to make the short walk into the hospital.

She knocked on the partially open door to his room. The requirements for visitor gowns and gloves had been lifted. Frank was sitting up in bed, his bandaged hands resting on a breakfast tray. The oxygen mask was gone as were most of the monitors. The room was oddly silent. He turned to her.

Loretta forced her best smile. "Looks like you're improving by leaps and bounds. How are you feeling today?"

Frank held her gaze. "I'm doing fine, physically. I'll be able to go home in a few days. The damage to my lungs wasn't as bad as they first thought, and my hands are healing well."

"That's great news," Loretta said, coming to his bedside. "Will you work from home? I can bring you what you need from the office."

"Maybe," he answered brusquely. "That's not what I wanted to talk to you about." He shifted his weight and leaned toward her. "You didn't take my advice and leave town with the kids."

Loretta wrung the purse's handle in her hands. "I couldn't leave you, Frank. The kids and I love you. I'm going to do whatever I can to make sure that you're safe."

Frank reached for her and pulled her close. "You can't do anything to make me safe, sweetheart. If you and the kids stay here and something happens to one of you, I wouldn't be able to live with myself. I love you, too, Loretta. I love you and the kids. In a perfect world, we'd be together forever. You're the family I've always wanted." He let go of her suddenly. "But this isn't a perfect world."

She turned her eyes to his and blinked back tears. "You're right; this isn't a perfect world. I can help—" she began, but he held up his hand to silence her.

"This isn't your mess to deal with; it's mine. I've done some terrible things, Loretta. Stupid things. You're not going to want to have anything to do with me once you know what I've done."

She opened her mouth to speak, but he shook his head and continued. "I got mixed up in the fraud that almost bankrupted the town and decimated the town workers' pension fund. I never intended to, but I should have known better. I've been working to restore everything that was lost, and I thought I could pull it off. But then Delgado got arrested, William Wheeler and Forest Smith died under suspicious circumstances, and now this," he said, holding up his bandaged hands.

Loretta remained silent, willing him to continue.

"I'm going to turn myself in. I've already talked to my attorney—we're going to do it later this afternoon. I'll turn state's evidence and try to negotiate a plea deal."

"Will you go to jail?" Loretta asked in a small voice.

"My lawyer thinks I will. I hope he's wrong. You need to know the truth. That's why you have to take the kids and leave town. Start your life over, somewhere safe. You're a terrific bookkeeper and office manager. You won't have trouble finding a new job." His voice caught in his throat. "And you're a beautiful woman, inside and out. You'll find a good man— not a scoundrel like Paul Martin or me—and you'll get married and lead a happy life."

Tears slid down Loretta's face.

Frank turned his face away from hers. "I'm so sorry that I disappointed you."

She shook her head. "That's not it. I'm not …"

"I don't deserve any favors from you, but I need to ask something of you before you leave," he said. "I need a jump drive from the wall safe in my office."

Loretta's pulse quickened.

"The safe is behind the picture next to my door and the key is taped to the underside of the lap drawer of my desk," he continued. "Bring the jump drive to me. David Wheeler is going to come see me today after school. He deserves to hear this from me before I turn myself in, just like you deserved to hear it."

She nodded.

"There's cash in the safe—almost a hundred thousand dollars. I want you to take all of it and get out of here. My funds will be frozen as soon as I confess, so I may not be able to help you after this." He reached for her hands and held them in his. "I promise you this: everything I own is yours if you ever need it. Will you do this for me?"

Loretta nodded slowly.

"Then it's time for you to go. And don't ever forget how special you are and how much I love you. If I could undo my mistakes, I would in a heartbeat. I'm so very sorry."

Loretta stepped toward the door and then stopped. "Nothing you've told me makes me love you any less, Frank. I don't want you to forget that."

Loretta returned to the hospital, now with two jump drives in her purse. She eyed the man in the business suit, typing on a laptop with a large briefcase open at his feet, as she passed the waiting room on the way to the nurses' station. The nurse on duty recognized Loretta and smiled. "Mr. Haynes already has a visitor with him and his attorney is in the waiting room."

"I have something he wanted me to bring him."

The nurse held out her hand. "You can leave it with me. I'll see to it that he gets it."

Loretta shook her head firmly. "I need to give this to him myself."

The nurse shrugged. "Suit yourself. You can go in there and wait with his attorney."

The man looked up from his computer screen as she entered the room. "Are you Loretta Nash?" he asked, setting his laptop aside and rising to extend his hand to her.

"I am," she replied, shaking his hand.

"Clark Bain. Mr. Haynes has told me a lot about you."

Loretta eyed the man warily.

"Were you able to find the item he requested?"

She nodded.

"You can leave it with me, if you like."

Loretta again shook her head.

"He's been with David Wheeler for the last half an hour. Frank's been discharged from the hospital. When he's done with David, I'm going to take him to his home. We'll meet with the authorities there." He looked at his watch. "He won't have time for you. Why don't you leave it with me? I'm assuming you've taken possession of the cash that Mr. Haynes provided for you?" Bain held out his hand for the jump drive.

Loretta stepped back, then turned and strode past the nurses' station and into Frank's room.

Frank was laying back against his pillows, ashen-faced. David Wheeler paced at the foot of the bed. He was gesturing wildly with his hands, and his voice choked with tears. "You lied to me. You pretended to be my friend, to be my father's friend. But you helped destroy him. You killed him, just like the others did. And you ruined my mother and me." He spun on Frank. "You're despicable, and I hope they put you away for the rest of your miserable life. I hate you."

Loretta made her presence known. "Frank is also the one who risked his life to save you from the fire." Frank and David turned to her. "I understand how you're feeling, David. But there are two sides to every story. He didn't wrangle your dad into participating in this. And he certainly didn't have anything to do with your father's death. Frank was as much a victim as your dad was. He genuinely cares for you and has been trying to help you. And he's been working to restore the pension fund."

"Then why's he going to the police if he's so innocent?"

"He doesn't want anyone else to get hurt." She gestured toward the hospital bed. "This has gotten out of control. Someone almost killed both of you."

Frank spoke up. "I understand your anger, David. I'm furious with myself. This is my own fault; my own greed and stupidity. Not a day goes by that I don't realize how many people I've hurt." Frank's voice cracked. "I hope that—one day—you can forgive me. You're a fine young man, and I've been proud to call you my friend."

David stopped pacing and looked at Frank. He shook his head. "I'm not sure what I think," he said. "I need to go." He moved to the door but stopped before he stepped into the hall. "Take care of yourself," he said over his shoulder as he stepped out of the room.

Frank sank back against his pillows.

"He'll come around, you'll see," Loretta said, approaching the bed.

Frank swiveled his eyes to her. "Did you bring the jump drive?"

She reached into her purse and withdrew the drive, placing it on the bedside table in front of him.

He picked it up, turning it over in his hand and examining it. He nodded. "Good. Thank you, Loretta." He turned his face away from her. "It's time for you to go. Don't forget what I told you. Have a happy life."

"I'm staying right here, by your side."

He looked at her. "I don't have time to argue about this. I need to get dressed and let my lawyer take me home. Maggie, Alex, and Chief Thomas will be at my house soon enough. You need to do as I asked and take yourself and your kids away from all of this."

Loretta was shaking her head as she opened the door to the tiny closet.

"The clothes are in that bag on the chair," he said, pointing to a shopping bag bearing the logo of a prominent retailer. "They had to cut my clothes off when I came in."

"Did that lawyer of yours bring you these?" She set the bag on the bed and began pulling items out and removing the tags.

"He did."

"I don't much care for his sense of style," Loretta quipped, holding out a shirt for him to put his arms through. "Will you need help with the pants?"

"I think I can manage them," Frank said, snatching them out of her hands. "You can go, now," he said with all the force he could muster.

"The only place I'm going is home with you and that lawyer of yours."

"There's nothing for you to do there. None of this involves you."

"Anything that involves you, involves me. I'll stay out of sight for your meeting, but I'm going to make sure you have something to eat and take your medication. The kids are spending the night with Mrs. Walters, and I'm going to spend the night taking care of you."

Chapter 30

Maggie and Alex rode to Frank's home together and parked by the side of the garage. Chief Thomas had texted that he was already there and his unmarked car was concealed in the garage. Another vehicle that Maggie thought might be Loretta's was parked at the front door.

They walked around to the rear of the house and the back door was opened by a tall man in a well-cut suit. "Clark Bain," he said, introducing himself. "Come this way."

Frank was ensconced in a recliner. He attempted to rise, but Maggie motioned for him to stay put. She came to his side and knelt down. "How are you, Frank?"

He shrugged.

"You saved our lives and almost lost yours. We're so grateful, and we're never going to forget that." She glanced at Alex over her shoulder. He nodded his agreement.

"Have you read what my attorney prepared?"

Maggie and Alex nodded.

"Did you understand it all? Do you have any questions?"

"We understood it, and we do have questions." Chief Thomas pushed himself away from the wall on the far side of the room.

"You thought that you were making legitimate investments?" the chief asked.

Frank nodded. "At first. Ron Delgado had advised me on my investments for years and had never steered me wrong. I was busy and didn't question things."

"You say 'at first.' When did that change?"

"Chuck Delgado started to gloat about his new portfolio and how it'd make him rich beyond his wildest dreams. I questioned Ron and learned that Chuck and I were the principal investors in the deal and that William Wheeler was part of it, too. I finally dug into the details and realized that what we were doing was fraudulent. The scheme was very sophisticated but we were, in essence, embezzling from the town and the pension fund."

"Why didn't you come to us then?" Chief Thomas asked.

Frank turned his head to one side, staring into the distance. "I didn't want to go to jail, and I thought I could fix it. If the recession hadn't hit, decimating property values, I would have been successful."

"So you've been working to correct the problem?" Maggie interjected.

Frank nodded.

"That's a convenient thing to claim now, isn't it? Now that you've been caught," Alex said.

"He hasn't been *caught*," Clark interjected. "He's come forward voluntarily, remember?"

Alex shrugged. "Do you affirm that the statements in this affidavit are true and accurate, based upon your personal knowledge and made of your own free will?"

Frank nodded vigorously. "Yes. It's all true." He reached into his pocket and pulled out the jump drive. He turned to Chief Thomas. "Here's the contemporaneous evidence that I talk about in my affidavit. I think you'll find this corroborates everything I've said." He sighed heavily and sagged back into his recliner. "Are you putting me under arrest?"

"They've agreed to make it look like you're under house arrest, for the time being," Clark interjected. "Partly for your protection. But it won't be long, considering your cooperation."

Alex wheeled on the man. "We've made no such agreement. We'll consider his cooperation and other mitigating circumstances *after* we've evaluated the information on that jump drive."

"That's not what we agreed to," Clark stated forcefully.

"It's all right, Clark," Frank said wearily. "I'm tired of trying to turn everything to my advantage. Delgado has to be stopped. We don't have time for you to enter into a lengthy negotiation."

"We'll be fair in our recommendations to the judge," Alex said, turning to Frank. "We'll get back to your attorney about all of this as soon as we can."

Chief Thomas stepped forward with an ankle bracelet. "I know I don't need to tell you this, Frank, but I wouldn't suggest going anywhere before letting us know. We can't risk losing you before this goes to trial. We have surveillance vehicles nearby. Call us if you see anything suspicious."

"That's it, then," Clark said, reaching into his briefcase. "Call me when you've got something to present." He handed each of them his card.

"Will you be all right here, tonight, Frank? Will you be alone?" Maggie asked.

"I'll be all right," he replied simply.

Maggie and Alex returned to his car, with Chief Thomas at their heels. She hoped that the car parked in front was indeed Loretta's. Whether he wanted to admit it or not, Frank needed help.

—⁂—

Frank dozed off after his attorney left. He was awakened by the aroma of chicken soup wafting to him from his kitchen. He stirred himself and padded into the room in his stockings. Loretta was busy portioning the soup into individual-sized containers for the freezer.

"Smells delicious," he said.

Loretta startled. "I didn't know you were awake, Frank," she said. "Didn't hear you come in."

Frank looked at the clock on the wall. "It's almost ten. I guess I slept through dinner."

"You can have some of this," she said, motioning him to take a seat at the counter as she set a bowl of soup, a spoon, and crackers down. "This will do you good. And it's time to take your medications. You don't want to take them on an empty stomach."

He picked up the spoon. "You don't have to ask me twice."

"How did it go in there?"

"You didn't try to hear any of it?" he asked, raising one eyebrow.

"I did try but couldn't hear very well. Are they being lenient because you are being helpful? Or will you go to jail?"

"Don't know yet. They've placed me on fake house arrest and set up surveillance. In spite of my attorney's advice to wait until we had a plea deal in place, I turned over everything I had. I have to do everything I can to get Delgado off the streets as soon as possible."

"That's the right thing to do, Frank. The honorable thing. I'm proud of you."

Frank put his spoon down and looked at Loretta intently. "That's the second time you've said that today. I don't know that anyone's ever said that they're proud of me." He turned aside. "No one's ever stuck by me like you have. I'm rich, and people are always glad to be along for the ride when times are good and cash is flowing, but they get scarce when the going gets tough."

"I'm not going to get scarce on you, Frank."

"You should take the money I left in the safe and leave town."

"That money is still in the safe, and I'm staying with you. Whether you want me to or not." She came to sit at the counter next to him. "Now, eat your soup before it gets cold. It's from scratch, and I put a lot of effort into it."

"On one condition," he said, turning to her and taking her hands into his.

"What's that?"

"That you do me the honor of marrying me when this is all over. If you still feel the same way. I don't want an answer tonight," he hastened to add. "You might feel differently if I go to jail. You might not want your good name tied with mine or your kids exposed to all this. But if you feel the same way when this is all over, I want to marry you."

"I'll give you my answer right now," she said, leaning her forehead against his. "I'm going to marry you. Whether you go to jail or not. I want to marry you now—as soon as you're well enough—before you go to jail if that's your fate."

Frank began shaking his head. "That wouldn't be ..."

Loretta put her fingers to his lips. "If you want it, you'd better put a ring on it, mister. We're going to get married, and we'll face whatever is in store, together."

"You don't know what you're agreeing to. You don't know what's on that jump drive."

Loretta swept her eyes over his face, then rose and retrieved her purse. She unzipped the inside pocket and withdrew her copy of the jump drive. He looked at her in confusion. She placed it in the palm of his hand.

"You're not the only one with something to confess," she said. She forced herself to look into his eyes. "I found that safe when you were hospitalized for your kidney stones." His eyes widened. "You know how snoopy I am." He nodded. "I found the key and opened the safe. You were acting so secretive that I knew you and Delgado were hiding something, and I was scared. I didn't know you then. I managed to copy the jump drive. It wasn't until much later that I began to understand what the figures on it meant."

"What were you planning to do with it?" Frank asked.

"If Delgado came at me, I was going to turn it in."

"Why didn't you? I was horrible to you after he tried to rape you. I still feel terrible about that, Loretta. It was despicable the way I treated you."

Loretta looked at her hands. "I went to Maggie with it right after that happened. Just like me, she was new to town, so she was the one person I knew who couldn't have been involved. But she threw me out on my ear before I could give it to her. I was so ashamed, I just left."

"I'm so sorry, Loretta. And after Delgado was arrested, why didn't you turn it in then?"

"I was afraid it also had information that would incriminate you. By then, I was falling in love with you and couldn't risk it. Until now—when Delgado tried to kill Maggie, Alex, and David. I knew I had to come forward to protect everyone."

Frank leaned back. "So you've known about me all along. You fell in love with me in spite of all this?"

Loretta nodded. "Are you mad at me for making this copy of the jump drive and concealing it from you?"

Frank looked at her for a long time, then slowly shook his head.

"You shared your secret with me, so I wanted to share mine with you. There have been enough things swept under the rug in my life. Not anymore. If you still want to marry me, knowing everything, then I sure as heck want to marry you," she said.

Frank pulled her face gently to his and kissed her.

Chapter 31

Aaron knocked softly on the bathroom door and pushed it open slowly. Susan was bending over the sink, splashing water on her face. She brought her gaze to the mirror over the sink and their eyes met. He raised an eyebrow and she nodded slowly.

Aaron let out a great yelp and lunged to circle her with his arms.

She put a hand on his chest and said, "Steady. Don't even think of picking me up and swinging me around." She pointed to the pregnancy test kit lying on the back of the toilet tank. "We're expecting. This is sooner than we'd planned. Are you happy?"

He took her face in his hands. "Are you kidding me? I'm overjoyed. Nothing could be better news. I'm sorry you've had morning sickness, but I'm glad you haven't had the flu. I was hoping for this."

Susan settled into his arms and nestled her head against his shoulder. "How long will this sickness last? I'm nauseated all the time. I swear I can smell the food inside of tin cans."

"It should clear up by the end of the first trimester." He kissed the top of her head.

"I hope so. I'm so sick I can't get to work before noon. I'm going to talk to my firm about taking another leave of absence."

He drew back and looked into her eyes. "If you're that miserable, why don't you resign from the firm and work from home assisting Alex? He told me he'd love to hire you full time."

Susan nodded. "I was thinking about that."

"You won't want to work the long law firm hours once the baby comes," Aaron said.

"Good point. Let me think about it. Right now, I want to try to eat some saltines and crawl back into bed."

"Can I talk to you about something else?" he asked.

Susan shook her head. "Not right now. I can barely keep my eyes open. Fatigue is part of this, too, you know."

Aaron walked her back to bed and tucked her under the covers. "I'll be right back with your crackers," he said. By the time he returned, Susan was sound asleep.

———

Aaron made sure that he had duplicate copies of his resume and transcripts in the folder for the recruiter. He felt bad about going to an interview Susan didn't know about. The opportunity had come up late yesterday afternoon. She'd been sound asleep by the time he'd finished his rotations at the hospital, and she'd been too sick and fatigued to hear about it that morning.

Still, he felt certain she'd be thrilled about this opportunity—especially now that she was expecting. Unless he misjudged his wife, she'd like nothing better than to live near her mother when they started their family. What an odd coincidence that this interview for a plum position had fallen into his lap the day before they'd learned she was pregnant. Or maybe it wasn't a coincidence after all.

He straightened his tie and got out of the car. He felt sure this was the right thing for his family and wanted to do his best during the interview.

———

Maggie was heading to her car in the college parking lot when she noticed the lanky figure of the college president approaching her. He raised a hand in greeting, and she did the same.

"Mayor Martin," President Lawry called. "I'm so glad I caught you."

Maggie extended her hand. "I was leaving early today," she said. "I'm usually here quite late."

"So I've heard," he replied.

"How can I help you?"

"You've done excellent work on the advisory committee," he said. "Even though you've only attended two meetings, your suggestions have been practical and actionable. We've moved along further on your recommendations in this short time than we have in the past year."

Maggie shrugged. "You're the chair of that committee. Any strides we're making are due to your leadership."

President Lawry shook his head. "Not so. Maybe at one time, but not now." He turned to face her. "As you probably know, I'm retiring at the end of the term."

Maggie nodded. "I'd heard that. I must say—I'm surprised. You're the most popular president of this college in recent memory, and it's obvious you enjoy your job. And you're way too young to retire."

"I'll be sixty-six next year," he replied. "But the real reason is my wife. Her health is deteriorating, and I want to spend as much time with her as I can. She's sacrificed a lot over the years to support me and my career. It's time that I look after her."

Maggie put her hand on his arm. "That's a lovely thing to do. As the former wife of a college president myself, I know firsthand the sacrifices she's made."

President Lawry smiled at her, and she detected sadness behind his eyes. "I didn't come here to tell you this. I came to ask you if you'd chair the advisory committee."

Maggie rocked back on her heels, shaking her head. "If I take on one more thing ..."

He put up a hand to stop her. "I thought long and hard about asking you, Maggie, for exactly that reason. But I've observed how much time and effort you're already putting into the advisory board. I've watched you around campus, interacting with students. You love it here; it gives you life." He held her gaze. "I know exactly how that feels. Truthfully, you won't be putting in any more effort chairing the committee than you are devoting to it right now."

Maggie drew in a deep breath. "You might be right about that."

"Don't make a decision now. Think about it, and talk it over with your husband. I have a feeling it'll be a good thing for you. I know it'll be a good thing for the college."

"All right," Maggie said slowly. "How's the search going for your replacement?"

"This is strictly confidential, but we've made an offer to a candidate and we're waiting to hear back."

"You don't sound terribly excited about the selection."

"Truthfully? The committee was more enthralled with him than I was, but I'm sure he'll be fine."

"Is there someone else you'd rather see take your spot?"

President Lawry produced an enigmatic smile. "Perhaps. Let's see if this candidate accepts the committee's offer."

Chapter 32

Maggie ambled across campus on her way back from the cafeteria the next afternoon. It was an unusually balmy day in early spring. Crocuses pushed their heads up through patchy clearings in the snow. She told herself to pick up the pace. Her inbox was full, and she had a least a dozen urgent matters to attend to, but she needed a break from it all. The investigators were still sifting through the information on the jump drive Frank had turned over to them. Both she and Alex were anxious and out of sorts, waiting for the results.

Her cell phone chirped in her purse with the ringtone that told her Susan was calling. She churned through the contents of her purse and scooped up the phone just before it went to voice mail.

"Susan," she said as she sidled over to a bench in the sun and sat down. "How are you, sweetheart?"

"Fine, Mom. Never been better."

"Are you over the flu?"

"Not exactly."

Maggie sat forward. "That's not good. I'm surprised you're not in the hospital."

"It's nothing to worry about. I didn't intend to scare you. I meant that I never had the flu …"

Maggie brought her free hand to her heart. "Are you …" she began.

"I most certainly am. You're going to be a grandmother again!"

"That's the best news I've had in ages!" Her voice caught, and before she could stop herself, she was crying. "When are you due?"

"October fourteenth," Susan said. "It's so early, we're not announcing yet."

"Okay," Maggie said. "I'll try not to give it away. Have you been to the doctor? Is it safe for you to be pregnant this soon after donating your kidney to Nicole?"

"The doctor told me it's fine. They'll want to monitor me more closely, but they expect me to have a normal pregnancy."

"How are you feeling?"

"Sick in the morning and tired all the time."

"I'm so sorry, honey. That's how I felt with both you and Mike. You'll get through it. The end result was worth everything I went through."

"I would hope so," Susan laughed. "At least I know I was worth it—I'm not so sure about that brother of mine."

"You know very well that you are both wonderful children and the light of my life." Maggie replied. "I wish I was nearby, so I could bring you chicken broth and crackers. And go shopping for the baby with you. I'll check my calendar, and schedule a week to come out to help you set up the nursery."

Susan remained silent.

"Unless you don't want me to." Maggie gulped hard. "Maybe you and Aaron want to do this on your own?"

"It's not that, Mom. Let's wait a bit on your trip out here," she said. "Until I'm feeling better."

"Good idea." Maggie replied. "What about your job? Will you work after the baby comes?"

"I'd like to go on a reduced schedule. I'm not sure my current job will allow me to do that. I may need to make some changes."

"You've got time to figure all that out," Maggie said. She checked her watch. "Sorry, honey, I'd love to keep talking, but I need to get going."

"That's okay. I'll see you soon," Susan said. "After we decide when you can come out here," she added hastily.

"Sure," Maggie said, furrowing her brow. One minute her daughter was delaying her visit and the next she was telling her mother she'd see her soon. She shook her head. What did it matter? Her daughter was pregnant—and Maggie was thrilled.

<hr />

John smelled the delicious aroma wafting from the kitchen as soon as he opened the back door. "Somethin' sure smells good," he called as he hung up his coat and bent to greet Roman and Eve, circling at his feet. "What's my gorgeous wife up to in the kitchen?"

"I'm doing a beef and broccoli stir fry," she answered as he swept her into his arms and kissed her.

"Smells amazing. You had an advisory meeting at the college today, didn't you?" he asked, cradling her in his arms.

"I did, as a matter of fact. How can you tell?"

"You're happy after those meetings, and you always come home and cook something wonderful."

Maggie laughed. "I'm not so sure about that, but we've had some fabulous news, and I'm celebrating."

"Do tell," John said, releasing her and heading for the uncorked bottle of wine on the counter.

She nodded as he held up a glass and poured.

"Susan and Aaron are pregnant," she blurted out.

His head came up. "I'm going to be a grandpa."

Maggie laughed, taking the glass he offered.

"Well … not really a grandpa. I know I'm not Susan's father," he added hastily.

"They'll think of you as a grandfather," Maggie said. "And so will this child. You'll be a better grandfather than Paul ever was." She raised her glass to him. "Here's to Susan and Aaron, and our first grandchild, together."

"And to the wonderful woman I was lucky enough to marry."

They drank their toast.

"This'll make for a very busy year. I'm sure you'll go to California to help her get ready. Will you spend time with her when she has the baby?"

"Of course. I've already penciled myself out of the office for two weeks in October. I'd like to take some long weekends this spring and summer to spend with her. I'm hoping you'll come with me."

"Won't I just be in the way?"

"Not at all. We'll have fun." Maggie turned the burner to low. "And with this new baby on the way, I'm not sure I'll have time to even sit on the Highpointe advisory board, much less chair it. I still haven't responded to President Lawry's request."

"You love that work," John replied. "When you come home from a meeting, you're so energized it takes you hours to relax."

"You think I should say yes?"

"To something that makes you that happy? I certainly do."

"It'll probably only be a temporary assignment anyway. When the new college president takes over, he or she will want to appoint their own chair to the committee. I'll be asked to step aside. I figure this is an interim appointment."

"Would you like to do it?"

Maggie nodded. "I really would."

"Then there's your answer. Everything will fall into place. You'll see."

"How did you get to be so wise?" She took a sip of her wine. "There's something about Highpointe that's so compelling to me. Being around the students is invigorating. I'll email President Lawry after dinner and accept."

John raised his glass to her. "To the new chair of the Highpointe College advisory board."

Judy Young glanced at the front of her shop when the bell tinkled, announcing that a customer had stepped inside. She leapt to her feet when she recognized that her visitor was John Allen.

"John," she called. "I don't think I've ever seen you in Celebrations during the middle of the day—unless it was an Easter carnival emergency. Which, I might add, went off without a hitch." She peered at him over her half-moon glasses. "Is everything all right?"

"Everything's terrific," he replied, surveying the displays for the section he was searching for.

"What can I help you find? Something nice for Maggie?"

John shook his head. "I'm here for a baby gift."

Judy took a step forward. "Who's having a baby? I generally know everyone around here who's expecting."

"I think they're keeping it quiet for a while yet, so I'd better not say. She's in her first trimester."

Judy eyed him closely. "All right then," she replied. There was more than one way to skin a cat. She'd figure this out based upon what he bought. "What were you thinking of?"

John held up both palms and shrugged. "I don't think I've ever shopped for a baby gift before. I have no idea."

"Do they have other children?"

John shook his head.

"Will you have to mail it to them?"

"I don't know."

"The baby section is over here," she said, motioning for him to follow her to a corner of the shop. "How much do you want to spend?"

"I don't have an amount in mind." He stepped to a display of handmade baby quilts. "These remind me of the blanket I had as a kid. I carried that thing around with me everywhere." He selected one that was pieced together in soft shades of yellow, green, and white. Silhouettes of dogs and cats were embroidered along the border.

"That's lovely, isn't it?" she smiled at him. "These are heirloom quality, and you've picked the most expensive one."

John handed her the blanket. "I'll take it."

"This baby must be very special to you." She eyed him closely. "Grandparents usually buy these."

John pretended he didn't hear her and turned to look through the discount items on the counter. Judy Young was like the town crier, and if he let the news of Susan's pregnancy slip out, she'd tell everyone.

"I'll gift wrap it. Do you want me to deliver it to Rosemont?"

John shook his head, making a show of looking at this watch. "I'll just pay you now and take it with me. I'm due back at the animal hospital in twenty minutes."

The door to Celebrations had barely closed behind him before Judy was on the phone to Joan Torres sharing her suspicion that Susan Scanlon was pregnant.

Chapter 33

Pete Fitzpatrick smiled as Maggie pushed through the door of Pete's Bistro shortly before seven. "Meeting the good doctor here for dinner?"

Maggie nodded. "How are you and Laura? And the baby? We've been busy, and it's been ages since we've been in."

"Everyone's fine. And we've missed you. Takeout is not the same, you know," he teased. "Let's put you in a booth by the window, so you can keep an eye out for John." He handed her a menu. "Specials are on the front. What can I get you to drink?"

"Just water, please."

"I would have thought you'd be celebrating," he said as he motioned to the server to bring Maggie a glass of water and returned to the hostess stand.

Maggie frowned. Whatever was he talking about? She scanned the list for the entree special and, not being a fan of liver and onions, opened the menu. She was struggling to read the small print in the dimly lit booth when a shadow fell across the menu. She looked up to find Nancy Knudsen.

"Hi, Maggie," Nancy said. "I don't want to interrupt. Tim's gone to bring the car around, so I thought I'd stop by on my way out to extend my congratulations." Nancy beamed. "That's such good news, and we're all thrilled."

Maggie raised her eyebrows quizzically.

"About Susan's baby, of course."

Maggie sat up straight and leaned against the back of the booth. "How in the world did you find out?"

"Judy Young spread the word. She said that John came into Celebrations today to buy a blanket for the baby. His first grandchild and all. Judy said he was really sweet."

Maggie shook her head. "We were trying to keep it quiet. She's only in her first trimester. And after Mike and Amy … well, we just wanted to wait a little while before we shared the news."

Nancy winced. "I'm so sorry. You know how this town is. Nobody can keep a secret to save themselves. And this is the best news we've had in ages. Everyone's so excited."

"You're right about that—it's wonderful news."

"I'm so happy for you, Maggie. We'll keep Susan and Aaron in our prayers. There's Tim," Nancy said, pointing to the car that was pulling to the curb outside the window. "I hope you're not mad that your secret is out."

Maggie smiled at her friend. "Not at all. Thank you for your well-wishes."

Nancy turned and exited the restaurant as John stepped through the door.

Maggie waved to him, and he made his way to their booth, a large Celebrations bag under his arm.

"You'll never guess what I did today," he said as he brushed her cheek with a kiss. He placed the package on the table between them. "I can't wait to show you what I got for the baby."

Maggie's heart swelled as she looked at her husband. "I can't wait to see what you've got in that bag."

John carefully pulled the quilt out and placed it on the table. "I had one sort of like this when I was little. I loved that blanket." He looked at her anxiously.

Maggie examined the fine piece of handiwork, admiring the stitching. She gathered the fabric in her hands and brought it to her cheek. "This is so soft!" she said. "You've made a wonderful choice."

John's countenance lightened. "I don't know what came over me. I had a break midday and made a beeline for Celebrations. I thought I'd bring this home to surprise you. If you don't like it or think Susan and Aaron won't like it, I can take it back and exchange it."

Maggie leaned across the table and kissed him. "It's perfect. I love it, and so will Susan. But most importantly, I'm sure our grandchild will love it."

John grinned. "I'm glad you approve. I was afraid that you wouldn't. And I was also worried that Judy Young might figure out why I was buying a baby quilt. I had to ask for the baby section, and she started drilling me with questions." He settled into the booth. "I found this one straight away, bought it, and got out of there before she could figure it out."

"About that," Maggie said, reaching over and patting his hand. "I'm afraid you weren't as discreet as you thought you were."

"Seriously? Why do you say that?"

"First Pete, and then Nancy Knudsen—you passed her on your way in—congratulated me."

John and Maggie looked into each other's eyes and burst out laughing.

"Judy can't keep a secret to save herself, but there's not a mean bone in her body," Maggie said. "I'll take that in a friend any day."

Chapter 34

David Wheeler collected the mail and tossed it onto the kitchen counter. He'd been back in school for a week and life had slowly settled back into a familiar routine. He dropped his backpack on the floor and bent a knee to greet Dodger. The dog accepted his master's ministrations, his tail beating a steady rhythm.

"When I finish my math homework, we'll go for a walk if it's still light out." Being locked in the Town Hall basement while a fire threatened his life had left him anxious and afraid. These days, even though he knew the police were keeping watch, he made sure he was home before dark.

David noticed his mother's note under a magnet on the refrigerator. She was getting her hair cut and colored after work and wouldn't be home until after seven. There was leftover lasagna in the refrigerator and bagged salad in the vegetable crisper.

Namor leapt onto the counter from his perch on top of the refrigerator. David scooped up the cat and held him to his chest, massaging Namor's back until the cat's body vibrated with his deep purr. When he'd finally had enough, Namor wriggled his way free. David retrieved the lasagna and warmed it in the microwave. He was on his way back to the refrigerator when he noticed the oversized envelope on top of the stack of mail. It was addressed to him.

The return address was from the law firm that had defended his father. He paused, then carefully opened the envelope and withdrew another envelope from the same law firm. The envelope was stamped undeliverable, addressee unknown. The postmarks showed that the envelope had been mailed and returned more than a year ago.

The microwave beeped, and the smell of cheese and marinara filled the room. David ignored it and took the envelope to the kitchen table and sat down. He opened it only to find a third envelope, addressed to the law firm in his father's unmistakable hand. David's breath caught in his throat, and he swallowed hard. The word *LEGAL* was scrawled across the envelope. This envelope had already been opened and he withdrew its contents: a single sheet of paper. A letter to David from his father.

He smoothed the letter on the table and leaned over it. The words swam in and out of focus and he blinked hard. He took a deep breath and began to read:

My dearest David,

If you are reading this letter, you know that I have taken my own life. I am so profoundly sorry for all of the pain, suffering, and humiliation I have brought on you and your mother. You need to know that none of this was either of your faults, and you are not to blame. You could have done nothing to prevent any of this.

By now you know all about the fraud and embezzlement and my part in it. I hope that they've convicted Chuck and Ron Delgado. They were the masterminds. I'm not sure about Russell Isaac. Frank Haynes and I were duped into going along with an investment scheme that we should have known better than to get involved in. By the time we figured out that what we were doing was illegal, it was too late—and too dangerous—to get out. I tried. That's why I think Delgado framed me for all of it. I was stupid, but I hope you believe I didn't intend to do anything illegal.

My life is over. I can't survive in prison. I want you and your mom to start again in a new town. Move away from Westbury to somewhere that your name won't be an embarrassment to you. You are a smart boy—way smarter than your old man. You won't make the mistakes in life that I've made.

You've been a wonderful son, and I'm extremely proud of you. You've got limitless ability. Go forth and live a happy life. Take care of your mom for me. If she meets a nice man who treats her right, encourage her. She's been a wonderful wife and deserves to be happy.

I hope you can forgive me for my shortcomings. My greatest joy in life has been being your father.

Love,
Dad

David pushed the letter away and pounded his fist on the table as tears rolled down his face. His shoulders heaved as he welcomed the release that the tears brought. Dodger pushed his head onto David's lap, and David buried his face in the dog's fur, drinking in the scent that was uniquely Dodger's. When his breath returned to normal, David pulled the letter back to him and read it again.

He was sitting at the table, staring at the letter with eyes that no longer saw it when Jackie Wheeler hurried through the back door. "David," she called as she entered the kitchen, "I forgot my checkbook. I'll just grab it and head back out to my hair …" She stopped abruptly when she saw him.

She ran to him and dropped to one knee. She placed her open palm against his forehead. "Are you feeling all right? You look like you've seen a ghost."

David turned wide, teary eyes to hers but didn't say anything.

"What's this all about?" She glanced at the letter that he clutched in his right hand. "What's that?"

David shrugged.

"May I?" Jackie asked, reaching for the letter.

He allowed her to take it from him. She slid a chair next to his, sat down, and began to read. A soft cry escaped her lips, and she put her hand over her heart. When she finished reading, she laid the letter on the table and looked at him.

"Where did you get this?"

David gestured to the envelopes spread out on the table. "It was in today's mail," he finally managed to say.

Jackie pulled the envelopes toward her and examined them. "It looks like this is real. Your father must have written this to you right before he—" Her voice caught. "He wanted to explain himself to you." She held up the envelope marked LEGAL that was addressed to their lawyer. "He must have included it in this envelope to his attorneys so that the prison guards wouldn't open it. He was relying on the attorneys to forward it to you."

She picked up the envelope bearing the rubber stamps. "They didn't have our new address after we lost the house, and so the letter bounced around for a while before it was returned to sender." She pointed to one of the stamped notations on the envelope. "The law firm finally sent it here."

"How'd they get the right address?"

"I called them last week to find out what legal fees we still owe them, and I gave them our new address."

"Did they mention the letter?" David asked.

Jackie shook her head. "Someone must have come across it in the file when they were updating our address and decided to stick it in the mail."

David nodded slowly.

Jackie leaned toward her son. "How are you feeling about all of this? It's a lot to take in."

"I don't know how I feel ... maybe a little mad that he didn't tell us this when he was alive. But relieved, too, I guess, to know that he didn't intend to do all those bad things." David let out a ragged breath. "I believe him— that he got caught up in something he didn't understand. Don't you?"

Jackie held his gaze and nodded firmly. "Even when I was angry with him for being arrested, I was always convinced he was innocent. Your father was a kind and generous man and would never have cheated and stolen from his friends and neighbors."

David leaned back in his chair. "This is what Frank was trying to tell me at the hospital. But I wouldn't listen. But hearing it from Dad ... I feel better. This helps." He picked up the letter and began to fold it.

Jackie patted his knee. "Keep that letter, David. It's yours. I don't think you need to turn it over to the police. There's nothing in there that will help them in their case against Delgado; they already know all that."

Jackie removed her coat and hung it on the hook by the back door. "I don't feel like getting my hair done tonight. Why don't I stay home and make us a decent meal? No leftovers tonight," she said as she reached for her cell phone and dialed her stylist.

A sense of calm descended upon David. He finished folding the letter, then zipped it into the interior pouch of his backpack. He knew who he'd go to with the letter.

Chapter 35

Frank roused himself from the recliner in front of the television set. He'd spent the afternoon dozing and now it was time to feed Sally, Snowball, and Daisy. He made his way to the kitchen and began to scoop food into their bowls as they circled excitedly at his feet. He placed the three bowls in their customary spots on the kitchen floor. Snowball tentatively picked at her food and Daisy approached hers in slow and steady fashion. Sally, however, devoured the brand of kibble that she ate every day of her life with relish. She was licking her bowl clean of every last morsel when her ears perked up, and she raced to the back door, barking and scratching to get out.

"What in the world?" Frank muttered as he made his way to the window in the breakfast nook. He peered through the blinds and saw a tall man in a dark hooded sweatshirt making his way across the backyard. Fear shot through him until he spotted the familiar dog at the man's side. Frank moved to the door and opened it to David and Dodger before David could raise his hand to knock.

"David," Frank said warily. "What are you doing here?"

"I have something I want you to see."

Frank stood motionless in the doorway, running his eyes over David's face. He nodded slowly.

Sally squeezed past Frank and pushed out the door, joining Dodger as they chased each other around the yard. Frank stepped aside and encouraged Snowball and Daisy to join them.

"We'll leave them outside to run it off." Frank motioned to the kitchen with his head. "Have you eaten?"

David nodded.

Frank walked to the kitchen table, rubbing his hands together. "How are you feeling? Have you recovered?"

"I'm fine," David said. "Still freaked out about the whole thing."

"Me, too. I'm not sure we'll ever get over it completely. The whole ordeal was horrible." Frank pulled out a chair from the kitchen table and sat down, motioning for David to join him.

David placed his backpack on the floor next to him. "I came over because I wanted to show you this." He unzipped the pouch and withdrew the letter. "I got a letter from my father in the mail today."

Frank jerked back. "What are you talking about?"

David recounted the explanation that his mother had put together based upon the rubber stamps on the envelopes.

"That seems possible," Frank replied, as he examined the envelopes that David passed to him. "I think your mother is right."

Frank's hand shook slightly as he took the letter that David handed to him. "Are you sure you want me to read this?"

David nodded solemnly.

Frank began to read. When he was done, he refolded the letter carefully and placed it on the table between them. He looked at David, then glanced aside, struggling to keep the emotion out of his voice. "Thank you for sharing this with me, David. I've thought about your dad every day since his death, and I've wondered why he took his own life, if there wasn't something I could have done to prevent it." He rubbed his hand over his eyes. "I'm so profoundly sorry that I didn't help him. I never wanted this for you and your mother."

"Dad thought that you were as much a victim as he was," David pointed to the letter. "Mom and I talked about it. They used both of you. Dad says he got caught because he tried to cut his ties with them. This isn't your fault, either," he said and his voice cracked. "The Delgados are responsible for my dad's death, not you. I know that now."

Frank blinked hard. He reached across the table and put his hand on David's arm. "Thank you, David. You can't know how much it means to me to hear this. I've made a lot of mistakes in my life, and it's now time I pay for them. I promise you that I'll spend the rest of my days putting things to rights."

"I hope you don't go to jail," David replied.

"I'm not sure the authorities feel the same way."

"You risked your life to save me and Maggie and Alex. Won't that count for something?"

Frank shrugged. "Maybe. I don't know yet. My lawyer is negotiating with them. We'll just have to wait and see." He sat back in his chair. "I'm really glad you came by tonight, David. If I go to jail, I'll need someone to help me. You're the only one I can ask."

"I'm not sure what I could do, but I'll try my best."

"I know you will," Frank patted his arm and released it. "You're smart and have a good head on your shoulders. If I go to prison, I'd like you to keep an eye on Forever Friends. You know as much about it as anyone. Make sure that things run smoothly and write to me immediately if there are any problems. Can you do that?"

David nodded.

"Loretta will manage Haynes Enterprises for me," Frank continued. "She's more than capable of doing that. I'm worried about her kids—especially Nicole. Loretta still has to watch her closely for any signs that she's rejecting the new kidney. She can use help with the kids, and they love you and Dodger. Plus, we've got Snowball and Daisy now. I talked Loretta into getting these dogs, and I don't want them to be a burden for her.

"I'll pay you for your time, of course, but would you keep an eye on them? Stay involved with the kids and help with the new dogs? Sean is interested in training Daisy to be a therapy dog, like Dodger, so maybe you could work with them."

"Of course I will," David replied. "They're great kids. That'll be fun for me. You don't have to pay me to do that—I'm not going to take your money."

Frank swallowed hard. "That's good of you. I'll never forget it, and I'll make it up to you, someday." Frank made a mental note to set aside some funds for David's schooling.

David looked into Frank's eyes. "Whether you go to jail or not, I'll help you."

Frank blinked rapidly. "The dogs will be getting cold by now. I'd better let them in." He moved to the door as David replaced the letter in his backpack.

Chapter 36

John Allen drove around the town square for the second time and stopped suddenly, allowing a car to pull away from the curb. He angled his Suburban into the newly vacated spot and turned to his wife.

"Parallel parking is one of your superpowers," Maggie observed.

"Thank you, madam. I hope it's not my main one?"

Maggie leaned toward him and kissed him leisurely. "Not at all," she replied when they pulled apart.

"Are you sure we have to make an appearance tonight?" he murmured as he traced a line of kisses along her jaw. "By the looks of the cars around the square, the place will be packed. They'll never miss us."

"It's tempting, I admit. I'm pooped and tried to get out of it when I left work tonight. I stopped by Alex's office to say that you were exhausted and we might not make it, but Alex insisted that we be here tonight. I've never seen him like that. So we can't be no-shows."

John sighed heavily. "You're right. I know Marc's worked long and hard on his new CD, and this launch party for it is important to him."

"We don't have to stay long. I told Alex that you're always in bed by nine on Friday nights."

"Just me? I don't believe I ever have to remind you that it's time for bed."

Maggie grinned sheepishly. "True enough, but using your spouse as an excuse to get out of something is one of the advantages of marriage."

John raised an eyebrow at her.

"We'll order dinner, and by the time we're done, Marc will have played his first set. We'll buy an armload of CDs and scoot out the door. We'll probably still be in bed before nine."

John opened her door for her and they strolled across the square, arm in arm, savoring the mild spring evening. The line of people waiting to be seated at Pete's Bistro was already out the door.

Pete spotted them as they approached and motioned for them to come to the front of the line. "Alex's saved you a seat at his table." He ushered them to a table for ten adjacent to the piano alcove. Tonya and George

Holmes, Tim and Nancy Knudsen, and Sam and Joan Torres were already seated and sharing a towering seafood appetizer.

Maggie and John circled the table, exchanging greetings with their friends before taking seats with their backs to the door.

"So where are Alex and Marc?" Maggie asked, turning in her seat to scan the crowd.

"We came in the rear entrance and saw both of them out back," Sam said. "Marc was pacing nervously, and Alex was trying to calm him down."

Tim checked his watch. "He's got almost an hour until he's supposed to play. Pete told me that Marc's going to start between the main course and dessert."

"I'm starved," George Holmes chimed in.

As if on cue, a waiter appeared at their table. "Do you need a few more minutes, or can I take your orders?"

George looked at Maggie and John. "They just got here, so ..."

Maggie broke in. "Start at that end," she told the waiter. "We'll be ready to order when you get to us." She opened a menu and shared it with John.

Thank you, Maggie, George mouthed across the table when the waiter retreated with their order.

The four couples relaxed into the easy flow of conversation between old friends. They had just been served their salads when a hush fell over the table. Maggie looked across at Tonya, then turned to see what had captured her attention. Maggie's fork dropped to the table, and she would have knocked her chair over in her haste to get up if Tim Knudsen hadn't reached out and caught it before it hit the floor.

Susan and Aaron were weaving their way across the crowded restaurant toward their table. Susan held out her arms and ran the last few steps to her mother. They circled their arms around each other and hugged tightly as Aaron and John shook hands. The two men stood back to smile at their wives' reunion.

"What in the world?" Maggie finally managed to say as she held her daughter at arm's length.

"It's quite a story," Susan said.

"Sit," Sam said, indicating the two remaining chairs at the table next to Maggie and John. He glanced at the others at the table. "I'm afraid I'm in on it."

Joan Torres drew back and looked at her husband in surprise. "You kept a secret from me?"

Sam put his arm around her shoulders and shrugged.

Susan turned to Aaron. "You tell them—it's your exciting news."

Aaron leaned across the table. "I finish my orthopedic surgical residency this June and have been looking for jobs. I had a preliminary interview with a large practice here in Westbury while three of their doctors were at a conference in California last month. They invited me to fly out here to see the practice and meet the rest of the doctors and staff."

The circle of faces around him nodded encouragingly.

"We arrived yesterday morning. I met with them in the afternoon, and we had dinner with the managing director of the practice and his wife last night. The practice is cutting edge; it's the preeminent orthopedic surgical clinic in the tristate area ..."

Susan put her hand on his arm and leaned across him. "They offered him the job this morning," she gushed. "And he's accepted. We're moving to Westbury!" She glanced at him sheepishly. "Sorry, sweetheart, you were taking too long."

Susan turned to her mother who was tearing through her purse, looking for a Kleenex.

Joan Torres reached across the table and handed her a small travel-size package of tissues. "Keep 'em. By the looks of you two," she said, smiling at mother and daughter who were now both crying, "you're going to need them."

"So I'll be right here when the baby comes, Mom," Susan managed to choke out. "We're having a baby," she said to the group at the table.

"We heard," Nancy said. "Congratulations, dear. We're all so happy for both of you."

Susan turned to her mother. "I thought we were going to keep it a secret."

"There's no such thing as a secret in Westbury, honey," Tonya said. "Your mom didn't say a thing. We're all as pleased as we can be."

"So who knew you were coming?" Maggie asked. "Why didn't you tell us?"

Aaron turned to Maggie and John. "Alex and Sam knew. We've been staying in a hotel room that the practice provided. It was my idea to keep this a surprise for you. I was pretty confident that I'd get the job. We knew you'd be at Pete's tonight and decided it would be fun to make our announcement here."

"That's why Alex was so insistent that we not back out tonight." Maggie leaned back in her chair.

"He called to tell me about that conversation." Aaron grinned at her. "You had us worried for a bit."

"When are you moving?" Tonya asked.

"We'd like to be here by the middle of June. I start work July fifteenth. The earlier Susan makes the move, the better. She's due October fourteenth," Aaron said. "I'll fly here with her, then Marc has agreed to come back to California with me, and we'll caravan to Westbury with our cars."

"You've got this all worked out," Maggie said. "What about your job, Susan?"

"I'll turn in my notice as soon as we get back. I'm going to work for Alex," Susan replied. "We'll list my place for sale by the end of the week. Homes in my neighborhood are going like hotcakes and mine has been updated, so it should sell right away. At least, that's what we're hoping."

"You can always stay with us at Rosemont," John said. "Until you can get settled in your own place."

"Thank you, John," Aaron said. "That'll depend on how hard it is to find a house here." He turned to Tim. "Can you help us with that?"

"You bet I can. We'll find you the perfect home for a growing family."

George Holmes signaled to their waiter. "We've got two more for dinner. Can you take their order? And bring us a bottle of champagne and some sparkling cider because we've got a lot to celebrate."

The waiter took the additional orders and retreated to the kitchen as Marc stepped onto the stage. The crowd erupted into applause. He bowed slightly and motioned for them to quiet.

"Thank you all for coming out tonight. As most of you know, Alex and I were seriously injured in an auto accident two years ago. We've both recovered physically, but that experience changed me. I appreciate the gift of life and notice the beauty of everyday things like I never did before. My new CD is a compilation of pieces I've done after the accident and reflect this new sensibility."

He paused and drew a deep breath. "I'm going to let my music tell the rest."

An anticipatory hush fell over the audience as he took his place behind the piano, raised his hands, and hovered momentarily over the keys. He lowered his hands, fusing his soul with the instrument and filling the room with his soaring music.

Chapter 37

Maggie sat at the farmhouse table in her breakfast room and smiled at John at the other end. The casserole dish containing her famous egg strata had been scraped clean, and only a dab of icing remained on the platter that had held her homemade cinnamon rolls. She relaxed in the satisfaction of knowing she'd served a meal that her family had loved. John nodded at her knowingly, as if he could read her thoughts.

She scanned the faces of Susan and Aaron seated on one side of the table and Alex and Marc on the other. The four young people were engaged in an animated discussion of Marc's new CD and speculating on the possibility of a Grammy nomination.

"His producer thinks he's got a lock on a nom," Alex said proudly.

Marc shrugged. "These things are very political. You never know. We'll just have to wait and see."

"You're being modest," Susan said. "You saw the reaction last night at Pete's."

"Those people are our friends," Marc replied, turning to nod at John. "You bought at least a dozen CDs. I want you to know how much I appreciate it."

"I bought that many because they're so good. I'm going to use them as gifts," John said. "Didn't you sell every copy you had on hand?"

Marc nodded.

"Three hundred," Alex interjected. "The vast majority were sold to strangers who wanted a copy—they didn't buy one just because they're your friends. And a lot of people did what John did and bought more than one copy." He looked at his partner. "I'm telling you what—I think you've made it to the big time."

Marc flushed with pleasure. "This is going to be a great year for all of us." He turned to Susan and Aaron. "We're excited about the baby and that you'll be moving to Westbury. I know that Grandma will want to babysit," he smiled down the table at Maggie, "but we want you to know that we're looking forward to spending time with the baby, too."

"That's awfully sweet of you," Susan replied. "You can come over to see the baby anytime you want."

"We mean it," Alex said. "We've already decided to turn the guest bedroom into a nursery for the little guy or gal."

"I've even Googled childcare classes and enrolled us in one at the hospital's birthing center. It's on how to care for a baby," Marc supplied. "Alex and I want to be great uncles. We're going to make sure we know what we're doing."

"You're serious about this, aren't you?" Aaron asked.

Marc and Alex nodded in unison.

John cleared his throat. "Maybe I should sign up for that class, too, since I've never had children of my own. A baby is different than a puppy or kitten."

Susan and Maggie exchanged surprised glances. "Looks like you're going to need a calendar to schedule babysitting time. You'll be lucky to have any time to spend with your own child," Maggie remarked.

"While we're talking about the baby," John said, rising from the table. "I bought something the other day. In fact, that's why word slipped out that you're pregnant." He looked at Susan and Aaron sheepishly. "It's all my fault, I'm afraid. I went into Celebrations and Judy Young somehow figured it out."

Susan grinned and leaned over. "It's all right. I don't know Judy well, but I suspect I wouldn't be able to keep a secret from her." She squeezed his hand.

"Thank you. Would you like to see what I got the baby?"

"Of course!" Susan almost squealed. "It'll be our very first baby gift."

John flushed, unable to conceal his pleasure as he headed toward the stairs. "I'll go get it. I hope you like it."

The grandfather clock chimed the hour in the background. "We have just enough time to open John's gift before we need to head to the airport," Aaron said.

"Are you sure you have to leave this morning?" Maggie asked. "Can't you change your reservation and go home tomorrow? Tim offered to take you house-hunting this afternoon—just to get an idea of what's available."

Susan shook her head. "We talked about that when we made our reservations. We need to go back to California to get my place ready to list and make arrangements for the move. We'll make a house-hunting trip later."

All heads turned as John entered the room carrying a Celebrations bag and an enormous stuffed bear.

Maggie burst out laughing. "I knew about Celebrations, but where did that bear come from?"

John shrugged. "I don't think I need to reveal my sources," he said, looking to Alex.

"Definitely not," Alex replied. "I instruct my client not to answer the question."

Susan stood and threw her arms around John. "You are the sweetest man on the planet, next to my own husband." She hugged the bear and took the bag from John. "Let's see what lovely thing you've got here," she said, pulling the quilt from the bag.

John leaned forward, anxiously searching Susan's face for her reaction as she stood and shook the folds out of the quilt.

"Would you look at this," she said, running her hand down the length of the quilt. "This is absolutely gorgeous." She turned to John, and her eyes were moist. "I love the yellows and greens; I'm doing the nursery in yellow and white. And these puppies and kittens along the border are precious. It couldn't be any more perfect." She picked up one corner of the quilt and examined it carefully. "This is handstitched, isn't it?"

John nodded as a smile flooded his face. "That's what Judy told me. Each quilt they sell is unique and made entirely by hand. They have others to choose from, so if you'd like to exchange it, feel free to pick one you like better."

"We love this one," Susan said, turning to Aaron. He nodded his agreement.

Susan swept John into a hug, the quilt sandwiched between them. "Thank you, John," she whispered in his ear. "You're going to be a wonderful grandfather to our baby. I'm so glad you and Mom found each other."

Chapter 38

Alex pushed the send key on the email to Phillip Hastings and shut his laptop. He looked at Chief Thomas and Maggie, who had been hovering over his shoulder, proofreading the email they'd spent the last hour and a half composing. "This will take some of the spring out of that pompous twit's step."

"The evidence that we're disclosing by this email proves Chuck Delgado is guilty," Maggie agreed.

"Thank God that Frank had that jump drive and turned it over to us. Everything we needed was on that drive," Chief Thomas said. "I wish we didn't have to disclose it to Delgado's attorney ahead of time. I'd love to spring it on them at trial—like on Perry Mason."

"Me, too," Alex agreed, "but you know the rules of evidence require disclosure. I can't do that."

"What do you think Hastings will do now?" Maggie asked.

"If he's smart, he'll get in here fast with an offer of cooperation and try to cut a plea deal." Alex replied.

"I don't want to give that bastard anything," Chief Thomas said. "We've got warrants out to arrest Ron Delgado and Russell Isaac. I'm assuming they're home in bed at this time of night. We should have them both in custody within the hour. I'll bet that they'll both want to turn state's evidence."

"We go from years of not enough evidence and not enough suspects to more than enough, all in a matter of a few weeks' time," Maggie observed. "Whoever would have thought?" She turned to Alex. "What do you want to happen?"

Alex leaned back in his chair and exhaled slowly. "If everything works out as I've envisioned, I'd have Ron and Russell both turn state's evidence in exchange for convictions on aiding and abetting charges—all felonies— with jail time of between five and seven years. They'd be eligible for parole in half of that time. I'd also require restitution of a million dollars each."

"Do you think that's likely?" Maggie asked.

Alex nodded. "I feel confident about them. Chuck Delgado's the wild card in this. Our new evidence is so strong that I think they'll be forced to plea. Hastings' team will know they can't win at trial, and he won't want a loss on his record."

"What do you think Chuck should get?" Maggie asked.

"The judge will insist on strict terms. Chuck could be sentenced to thirty years, without the possibility of parole, and should be ordered to reimburse the pension fund the forty million he stole, plus interest and penalties."

"Seems reasonable to me," Maggie said. "At his age, it's likely to be a life sentence."

Chief Thomas nodded. "That's just for the fraud and embezzlement charges. If the evidence that the feds are gathering establishes that he set the fire at Town Hall, they'll charge him with that, too. And if Ron or Russell produce testimony that links Chuck with the arson fires several years ago or with Alex's near-fatal car accident right before the last election, we'll bring him in for arson and attempted murder."

Maggie crossed her arms in front of herself and began to pace. "What about Frank? Have you decided what to offer him?"

Alex eyed her closely. "You want him to get off easy, don't you?"

Maggie shrugged. "I believe in redemption. I know he did some bad things after he learned that his 'investment' was really a criminal enterprise. He shouldn't have tried to cover up his involvement, but he also tried to make things right. And he came forward voluntarily with the evidence we needed. He's a changed man." She stopped in front of Alex and looked into his eyes. "He risked his life to save both of us and you know it."

"I'm not supposed to let personal feelings influence my judgment," Alex said. "I may have to recuse myself and let someone else work on his deal."

"Let's get the other three settled, first," Chief Thomas said. "I think we should also put out a statement clearing William Wheeler. He was duped, too."

"I've already got one drafted," Alex said. "His family has suffered enough."

"That'll help David a lot," Maggie replied. "You know, I thought I would feel euphoric when we finally had the evidence to nail these guys. Now that we do, I'm relieved, but I don't feel like celebrating. I thought we'd open a bottle of champagne or something, but all I want to do is go home and crawl into bed."

"It's almost one in the morning," Alex said. "That may explain it. We've been running on empty for months. I feel the same way."

"There'll be plenty of time to celebrate when these guys are behind bars. Plus, we still need to restore the stolen funds to the pension fund and the general fund. The fines that we're going to levy may never be paid," Chief Thomas said. "I'll drink a toast when we've righted all the wrongs." He pointed to Maggie's coat hanging on the hook by the door to her office. "I'm going to follow you home and make sure you get safely inside Rosemont. Tomorrow will be another busy day, and we'd better get some sleep."

Chapter 39

Maggie nodded at Chief Thomas as she and Alex joined him outside her office later that week. "You were certainly right about how busy these last few days were going to be," Maggie said, glancing at the chief over her shoulder.

"After all these months, struggling to build our case against these guys, it's hard to believe that it's almost all over with," Alex replied.

"I was surprised how quickly Ron and Russell turned state's evidence," Maggie remarked.

"They'd already discussed it with their respective attorneys," Chief Thomas said. "That's why it all came down so fast."

"Ron and Russell provided more evidence than we expected," Alex said. "We were lucky that the jump drive contained what we needed to arrest them."

"I'm glad we can give the public some good news for a change," Maggie said as they started down the stairs. The press conference in the lobby of Town Hall was scheduled to start in a few minutes. "Do you think the agreed-upon sentences will satisfy the public?"

"Ron and Russell are both getting jail time and hefty fines, which they've made arrangements to pay," Alex said. "Some people will think they're getting off too easy. But Chuck Delgado is getting thirty years without the possibility of parole and a fine in excess of sixty million dollars, including interest and penalties."

"It was gratifying to take him into custody this morning," Chief Thomas said. "His attorney dropped him off at the jail like he was taking out the trash. Hastings handed over the paperwork and was out the door without a backward glance. Chuck's lost all of his swagger. He looked terrified."

"Was Bertha with him?" Alex asked.

"I heard she's filed for divorce and moved out of state," Chief Thomas said.

"We're only discussing the three of them," Maggie said. "We're not making any statements about Frank or what his sentence might be."

"Agreed," both men replied in unison.

"Let's enjoy this moment; we've worked very hard for it."

———

"President Lawry," Maggie said into her cell phone, sinking into the over-stuffed chair in the library. She leaned forward and released the latch on the French doors, opening them to the balmy spring evening. Rosemont's back garden was thick with the shadows of the approaching dusk. Bird song filled the air.

"Mayor Martin," he replied. "I hope I'm among the first to congratulate you on today's news. Justice has finally prevailed. I'm delighted."

"Did you see the press conference?"

"Of course. We had it on the big television in the lobby of the admin-istration building. There must have been two hundred people gathered to watch. You should have heard the applause when you were done."

Maggie kicked off her shoes and tucked her feet up under herself. "That's awfully nice to hear. I hope the rest of the town feels that way."

"You can count on it. Everyone's all abuzz. You should go out some-where tonight; soak up the praise and congratulations."

Maggie covered her mouth with her hand, stifling a yawn. "Frankly, I'm so exhausted, I'll be lucky if I make it upstairs to bed before I fall asleep."

"I can imagine," he said. "Then let me get to the other reason I'm call-ing. I'd like to invite you to be our commencement speaker."

"I thought your new president was going to speak."

"He was, but something's come up, and he won't be able to attend. I know this is incredibly short notice," President Lawry continued, "com-mencement is a week from Friday. You delivered such a welcome message when you were on that panel. You spoke to those kids about crafting a hopeful future, and you do the same when you talk to students around campus. You may not know it, but ever since you've been working out of the temporary Town Hall on campus, you've been the talk of the place. The student body and the faculty love you. When our new president bowed out, you were the committee's unanimous choice."

Maggie inhaled slowly. Her brain was telling her she should decline—the last thing she needed was to prepare a commencement address in only two weeks' time. "I'd love to," she heard herself saying.

President Lawry released the breath he had been holding. "Thank you, Maggie. You'll do a spectacular job. I'll send you an email with all the details."

"The new president is still going to be the new president, right? He's just canceling out of the commencement address?"

"No. Confidentially, Maggie, we found something negative in his background check and we rescinded our offer."

"That's unfortunate. What are you going to do now? Will you stay on for a while longer?"

"We've got another candidate in our sights."

"Good," Maggie said, and this time she was not able to stifle her yawn.

"Good night, Maggie. And thank you, again, for stepping into the breach. I'll see you soon."

Chapter 40

Maggie woke before her alarm went off on the morning of graduation day. She slipped quietly out of bed, roused Eve from her slumber in her basket in the corner of their bedroom, and tiptoed to the hallway. John had taken the day off to attend the ceremony, and she didn't want to wake him on one of the rare mornings when he was able to sleep in. Susan and Aaron had flown in the day before to hunt for a house. Rosemont would soon be bustling with activity. She wanted to enjoy a few moments of early morning solitude.

Roman greeted her at the top of the stairs, and they headed for the kitchen. She fed the dogs and made herself a cup of coffee while they ate. When the dogs had finished, she picked up her coffee mug and her notes for her speech and padded out to the back garden. The dogs raced ahead of her, leaving paw prints in the dewy grass.

Maggie paused at the edge of the patio, looking down the sloping expanse of grass to the low stone wall that separated the lower lawn from the swath of woods at the bottom of the property. She stood and sipped her coffee, watching the sun rise over the tops of the trees; painting the lawn in a shimmering blanket of early morning light. Roman raced back to her, barked twice, and then took off after Eve.

She set her empty coffee mug on a nearby table and picked her way down the lawn to the stone wall. She arranged her notes on the wall, treating it like a podium, and straightened herself, staring into the stand of trees beyond.

Maggie cleared her throat and began her speech. Having her notes in front of her was reassuring, but she was gratified to find she didn't need them. She delivered the final line of her speech and spun around quickly at the sound of applause coming from behind her.

"That was brilliant, Mom," Susan said, smiling at her mother and clapping. She cocked her head to one side. "I always thought of Dad as the public speaker in the family. I've never heard you do more than a press conference. That was inspirational. Truly."

"For heaven's sake," Maggie said, breathing hard. "You scared the life out of me. I didn't hear you come up behind me. How long were you there?"

"Long enough to know that I'm glad I'll be there later to hear the whole thing," Susan said.

"Are you sure, honey? It's at eleven o'clock. That's right in the middle of the day—hardly convenient for the two of you. You made the trip to house-hunt, not hear me deliver a commencement speech."

"We wouldn't miss it," Susan assured her. "We're meeting Tim Knudsen at seven-thirty for breakfast to go over the listings he's pulled for us. We're also going to meet with his mortgage person to fill out paperwork for loan prequalification. He's going to drop us at the college at ten thirty and pick us back up at one to go look at the houses we selected at breakfast."

"Sounds like a good plan. I hope you find something today, but don't worry if you don't. You can always stay here at Rosemont until the right house comes along."

"I'm sure it won't come to that," Susan put her arm around her mother. "But I think you'd like to have us here for a bit, wouldn't you?"

Maggie leaned in and kissed her daughter's cheek. "Is it that obvious? I'd love to have you bring my grandchild home to Rosemont."

"We'll be in the same town. You'll get to see the baby all the time, regardless of where we live." Susan glanced at the house in time to see Aaron step out the backdoor and wave to her.

"We'd better get back up there. What are you going to do until it's time to leave for the commencement ceremony?"

Maggie smiled at her daughter as they made their way up the sloping lawn. "I'll probably spend the morning redoing my hair and makeup in a nervous frenzy. At least I'm wearing a cap and gown, so I don't need to worry about my outfit."

"I've never seen you in academic regalia, Mom." Susan stopped and turned to face her mother. "I'm so proud of you. You're the inspiration for how I live my life. These kids are lucky to be able to hear your message today. Knock 'em dead."

"Are you ready, sweetheart?" John called as he ascended the stairs. "We'd better get going."

Maggie stepped out of their bedroom in her academic gown, her purse in one hand and her cap in the other.

John stopped on the top landing and whistled. "You look absolutely gorgeous and incredibly imposing, all at the same time."

"For Pete's sake," Maggie said, blushing. "Nobody looks good in one of these hideous gowns."

John walked down the steps with her. "You do. It suits you."

"Thank you. I just hope I don't let them down."

"You won't. I listened at the door while you were rehearsing." Maggie rolled her eyes at him. "It's a terrific speech. Those kids—and their parents—will remember it for years." They reached his Suburban, and he held the door for her. "I'm incredibly proud of you."

They rode the short distance to Highpointe College in silence.

As she chatted with the faculty and staff before the ceremony started, Maggie's mind wandered back to the decades she'd spent in this situation as a college president's wife. She shook her head slowly. How different her life was now. She had never imagined herself in the role of commencement speaker.

President Lawry touched her elbow.

"It's time to join the procession," he said as the familiar strains of Pomp and Circumstance filled the air. She lifted her face to his and took a deep breath. He looked at her closely. "This feels like home to you, doesn't it?"

Maggie nodded. They turned, and she followed him from behind the heavy crimson curtains onto the outdoor stage. She took her place next to him and surveyed the crowd; happy graduates in caps and gowns in the center front section, flanked by proud families on either side. She nodded slightly when she picked out John, Susan, and Aaron in the bleachers to the right, then forced her attention to the remarks that President Lawry was making. She felt a rush of adrenaline as he finished her introduction, and she stepped to the podium.

Maggie glanced at the pages in front of her, then looked up at the faces turned to her. She didn't need her notes. Everything she wanted to say was written on her heart. She thanked President Lawry for the opportunity to be with them on such an auspicious occasion and congratulated the graduates and their families. "Preparing this address has given me the opportunity to examine my own life—my own successes and failures—as I've tried to distill the best advice to give you as you begin your journeys into your adult lives. You'll make mistakes, as we all do, and if you're smart, you'll take the lesson from those mistakes without letting them derail you. I have three principles that have proved very helpful in my own life: set your bar high— make sure that your goals are worthy of your efforts; be true to your personal values and guard your integrity; and as my grandmother used to say, 'Don't borrow trouble or *horribilize* over problems that haven't happened yet.' Let me elaborate …"

Maggie finished her address thirty minutes later and the crowd leapt to their feet in an enthusiastic ovation. Maggie moved back to her seat as President Lawry stepped forward to award diplomas. "Well done!" he leaned in to whisper as they passed each other.

The reception after the commencement ceremony went by in a blur. Maggie was surrounded by students and parents, pumping her hand and requesting pictures with her. She caught Susan's eye as they tried to make their way to her through the crowd. Maggie shook her head and motioned for them to head to the parking lot. Susan smiled in acknowledgement and turned away.

By two o'clock, the last of the participants had departed. Maggie found John waiting patiently, sitting in one of the chairs that earlier that day had held a new graduate. She sat down next to him.

"You did a remarkable job with that speech." He looked at her intently. "The crowd was electrified. You felt it up there on the stage, didn't you?"

"I did." She turned to face him. "This is an experience I'll remember for the rest of my life. I'm so glad I agreed to do this." She got to her feet. "I'm sorry that this has eaten up your whole day. Are you ready?" she asked.

"I wouldn't have missed this for the world. You've got one more thing to do before we leave. President Lawry told me he'd like a word with you before we go," John said.

"Okay." Maggie unzipped her gown. "This thing is getting hot. He's over there," she said, pointing to a group of people. "Let's go see what he needs and then head home."

Maggie made her way to where President Lawry was standing, his back to her, with the board of trustees gathered around him. One of the trustees pointed to her as she approached, and the president turned to her.

"Maggie," he said, extending his hand. "On behalf of Highpointe College, the Board of Trustees thanks you for delivering one of the most memorable commencement addresses in our history."

"Thank you very much. It was my pleasure. John and I are headed home, and I want to thank you for the opportunity ..."

President Lawry held up a hand to stop her as one of the trustees handed him a thick envelope. "We have another matter we'd like to discuss with you." He straightened and held out the envelope to her. "On behalf of the Board of Trustees of Highpointe College, we'd like to offer you the position of president. We are convinced, today more than ever, that you are the perfect candidate to lead this prestigious institution."

Maggie stared at him, mouth agape, as she took the envelope from his hands.

"The details of the offer are in there," he said, nodding at the envelope as he released it to her. "We realize that this must come as a tremendous surprise." President Lawry looked into her eyes. "I've never been sorry, for even one day of my life, that I've spent my career serving this institution. I believe that you'd be as happy here as I've been. I feel certain that you know, in your heart, that this is the place for you." His voice broke as he continued. "You can impact a tremendous number of lives as president of this college. Even when we made the offer to that other candidate, I felt that you would have been a better choice. So please take this home: talk about it with John; think about it; imagine yourself in this role. If you have any questions, please call me. Any hour of the day or night. Your term as mayor is almost up; you could start when your successor is sworn in."

Maggie nodded as she looked at each of the trustees in turn and a smile spread slowly across her lips. "I'm honored. I promise I'll think about it."

Chapter 41

Loretta placed her hand on top of Frank's as it rested on his computer keyboard. "Enough. We've gone over and over these reports. I've got it."

Frank nodded slowly and turned to her. "I just want to make sure that you know as much about running Haynes Enterprises as you possibly can."

"You're still going to be running it, Frank."

"We don't know that, Loretta. My attorney isn't holding out much hope that I'll get off without significant jail time." He looked into her eyes, and she recognized his steely resolve. "I have to make sure that you can keep things going, so that you and the kids are taken care of. You're on all of the bank accounts now, and I want you to take whatever you need."

Loretta swallowed the lump in her throat. "That's incredibly kind of you, Frank."

"I love you, Loretta. You and the kids. The thought of being away from you is killing me."

"We don't know you're going anywhere, yet. Let's deal with that if it happens."

"Clark says we should know something next week. I want to get everything done before Monday, so we'll be ready."

"There's one more thing I'd like to do to get ready." Loretta cupped his face in her hands.

He raised an eyebrow.

"I'd like to marry you, Frank. Now."

Frank pulled back and began to shake his head. "We talked about this before. You don't want to be saddled with me ..." he began.

"We did talk about it. And I said that I'm sticking with you, no matter what. It would be the greatest honor of my life to be your wife." She paused and held his gaze. "And if I'm your wife, I'll have enhanced rights with both the business and to visit you in prison—if that's necessary." She could see that her remarks hit home. "I love you, Frank."

Frank nodded and a smile spread across his face. He pulled her to him and kissed her, a long kiss full of yearning. When they parted, he whispered in her ear. "The honor would be all mine."

Loretta rested her forehead against his. "If you really think you'll be sentenced next week, let's get married Monday. By the town clerk."

"Are you sure you don't want to wait to have a big wedding?"

"I'm sure. The kids get out of school at two-thirty. Let's get married at four o'clock."

"Four o'clock Monday it is. You and me and the kids. Is there anyone we should ask to be our witness?"

"David," they both said in unison.

———

Sean Nash raced up the steps to Haynes Enterprises, his dog Daisy at his side. Marissa and Nicole followed at a more leisurely pace with Snowball, while David and Dodger brought up the rear.

"Mom," Sean said as he barged through the door. "You should've seen us! Daisy's doing great. David says he's never seen a dog learn so fast. Even Dodger." He came to a halt at the door to Frank's office where Loretta and Frank were still seated, discussing their plans for Monday afternoon.

"That's terrific news," Frank said, getting up and coming to greet them. "I'm not a bit surprised. You're a natural with dogs," he said, patting Sean on the back.

Sean beamed.

"Did you have fun?" Loretta asked the girls.

"So much fun," Marissa said. "Snowball did good, didn't she? She's really smart, too." She looked at David.

"She sure is," David replied. "You've got two great dogs. If you work with them at home, like I showed you, they could both become therapy dogs."

Frank came forward and clapped David on the back. "That's great news. You're a wonderful teacher, David."

"Can we go get lunch now?" Nicole asked, looking up at Frank. "I'm hungry."

"In a minute," Loretta said. She glanced at Frank. "We have something we want to tell you." She motioned to the sofa along the wall in the reception area. "Sit down."

The children did as they were told, the two dogs at their feet. David turned to leave.

"We'd like you to hear this, too, David," Frank said.

David and Dodger sat on the floor next to the couch.

Frank put his arm around Loretta's shoulder and began. "You know that I love you and your mother very much."

"And I love Frank," Loretta said, looking at her children. "I know you love him, too."

"We've decided to get married." Frank paused to let his words sink in.

The three earnest faces stared at them in silence until Nicole got off the sofa and came to Frank. She circled him with her arms. "I prayed that you'd be my daddy someday."

Frank knelt and scooped her into his arms, struggling to hold back tears.

The other two children followed their sister and the soon-to-be family swayed in a group hug. Frank lifted his head to look at David.

"Congratulations," David said. "I'm happy for all of you."

"There's something else," Frank said as he pulled away and turned to David. "Loretta and I would like you to be our witness."

"Sure." David furrowed his brow. "What's a witness?"

"You'd sign the official wedding certificate for the legal records." Frank put his hand on the boy's shoulder. "You'd be my best man."

David smiled broadly. "I've never been a best man. That'd be cool. Do I need to wear a tuxedo?"

Loretta shook her head. "Whatever you wear to school will be fine."

"When're you getting married?"

"Monday. Four o'clock, at the town clerk's office."

Chapter 42

John stepped through the back door of Rosemont that Saturday morning after taking Roman for a brisk jog. He toweled the sweat from his brow with the hem of his shirt while Roman headed straight for the water bowl. Maggie sat at the farmhouse table with two kitchen drawers set out on the table in front of her, their contents strewn about. Eve was curled into a ball, snoozing at Maggie's feet.

John stopped short at the sight of his wife. "We haven't been married that long, but I know what this means," he said gesturing to the table.

Maggie grabbed Bubbles, who was batting at a skein of kitchen twine that had come from one of the drawers, and bent over to set the cat firmly on the floor. Bubbles jumped back onto the table before Maggie straightened up. "And what does my beloved husband think this means?"

"You're deep in thought. Trying to decide if you want to trade in being Mayor Martin for President Martin?"

"Right you are," Maggie said, scooping up Bubbles again. "Organizing drawers always helps me think."

"By now," John observed, "I wouldn't have thought we had any drawers left to organize.

Maggie smiled at him. She began putting the items back into the drawers. "I know what I want to do. In my heart of hearts."

"Congratulations, President Martin," John said, moving to her side and bending to kiss her.

"Is it that obvious?"

"It is to me. You're perfect for the job, and it'll make you happy. What more is there to say?"

"Plus the money is so much more than I'm making now. We'll be able to pay the taxes on all the silver we sold last year in order to buy out Frank's interest in Rosemont."

"That's another good thing. There's no reason to turn it down."

"Except my duty as mayor to see things through and get Westbury back on track."

"You've brought the bad guys to justice and have made terrific strides forward on the town's finances. You don't have to do everything, you know," he said. "Someone else can finish this up."

"I'm sure you're right about that." Her cell phone dinged, signaling that she'd received a text message.

Maggie picked up her phone. "It's Susan," she said, looking at John. "They've narrowed it down to two houses. They wonder if we can join them at Pete's for lunch and then go see both choices. They'd like our opinion before they make an offer."

"You put those drawers back together while I race upstairs for a shower. I bet I'll be back down before you can finish."

"You're on," Maggie cried, reaching for a wire whisk as John bounded up the stairs.

———

John settled the bill as Maggie and Susan made their way back to their table from the ladies' room. They were passing the entrance when the door opened and Loretta and her children walked into the restaurant, followed by Frank and David.

"Susan!" Nicole cried, rushing to her.

"Hey, sweetie," Susan said, dropping to one knee to greet her sister. "How's my girl?"

"We've got big news," Nicole said breathlessly. "Frank is gonna be my daddy."

Maggie and Susan turned to Frank and Loretta, unable to mask their surprise.

Frank cleared his throat. "Loretta and I are getting married."

A wave of happiness washed over Maggie. She stepped toward the couple, opening her arms and embracing them both. "That's wonderful." She leaned back and looked into Frank's eyes. "I couldn't be happier for you."

"When are you getting married?" Susan asked.

"Monday afternoon. At the clerk's office. We'll pick up the kids after school and head to Town Hall. It'll be a very simple wedding," Loretta said.

"I'm going to be the witness and the best man," David supplied proudly.

"That's wonderful," Maggie said, smiling at the boy.

Loretta turned to Susan. "What are you doing in Westbury?"

"We sold my place in California and came to do some house-hunting," Susan said. "That's why I didn't call you." Susan hugged Nicole. "This is a busy trip already, and we'll be moving here in a couple of weeks. I can spend time with you then."

"Have you found anything?" Loretta asked.

"Maybe," Susan replied. "We've narrowed it to two, and we're taking Mom and John with us this afternoon to see them again." Susan looked at her watch. "And we're late."

"Don't let us keep you," Loretta said. "And good luck."

"May I come down to the clerk's office on Monday afternoon to see you get married?" Maggie addressed her question to Frank.

Frank swallowed the lump in his throat. "Of course you can, Maggie."

"I'll see you Monday afternoon," Maggie said to the couple. "I'm delighted for all of you."

———

"She's over there," John said, pointing to Judy Young the next morning after the eleven o'clock church service concluded.

Maggie caught Judy's eye and nodded to her. She and John wove their way through the crowd to join her.

"I hear you've got big news," Judy said.

Maggie and John exchanged a glance. "What would that be?" Maggie asked.

"I hear Susan and Aaron put in an offer on one of those model homes on the outskirts of town—that big craftsman-style house with five bedrooms and all the gorgeous woodwork."

Maggie laughed. "That's the one. Have you been through it?"

Judy nodded. "I tour all the models. Even though I'm not in the market to buy a new home, it gives me great ideas. Sometimes I buy things for Celebrations based upon what I see in the models. I've gotten some of my bestsellers that way. You'd be surprised."

"You are one sharp businesswoman," John chimed in.

Judy blushed, obviously pleased by his remark. "It's time for us to plan Susan's baby shower," Judy said. "Is that what you wanted to talk to me about?"

Maggie shook her head. "I agree that we need to plan the shower, but I've got another event in mind, first."

Judy arched an eyebrow. "Spill the beans."

"What would you say to a wedding at Rosemont tomorrow afternoon?"

"I'd say yes. Definitely yes. Who's getting married?"

"Frank and Loretta."

Judy took a step back. "No kidding." She paused, letting the unexpected news sink in. "Well … how about that? I never thought I'd be happy for Frank Haynes, but I am. He's not the same self-centered guy he used to be." She scanned the crowd and her hand shot in the air when she found who she was looking for. Judy motioned to Joan Torres to join them.

"We've done weddings on short notice before, remember? If we can throw Susan a wedding at the hospital, we can do this," she said to Maggie.

"Wait until you hear what we're going to be working on this afternoon," Judy called to Joan as she approached. "It's right up our alley …"

Chapter 43

"Why are we going this way?" Loretta asked Frank on Monday afternoon as they pulled out of the school parking lot with all three children buckled into the backseat. "Town Hall is temporarily at Highpointe College, which is in the opposite direction."

"David called me at lunchtime. You'd already left to get your hair done. Sorry I didn't tell you. He had to go by Rosemont right after school to help Sam Torres unload lumber. David asked if we could pick him up there."

Loretta sighed heavily.

"Maggie and John will be at work. He'll be waiting in front. You won't even have to get out." He reached over and took her hand and brought it to his lips. "You look breathtaking," he said, glancing at her.

"Thank you," she said, relaxing back into her seat as they turned onto the long, winding driveway to Rosemont.

Frank made the final turn and Rosemont came into view, its limestone facade glowing in the late afternoon sunshine. The driveway was lined with parked cars. Loretta turned to Frank. "What's going on?"

Frank shrugged. "I honestly don't know. David said he'd be waiting outside."

Frank drove slowly to the entrance. The railing by the steps was festooned with white satin ribbon tied at intervals with enormous bows. The mahogany front door was decorated with a swag of white and cream flowers composed of roses and tulips, lilies and baby's breath. The town clerk smiled at them from the bottom step as they stopped in front of her.

"Good afternoon, Mr. Haynes," the clerk said as Frank rolled down his car window. "We've had a change of venue. The clerk's office is operating out of Rosemont for the rest of the afternoon."

The clerk bent down, so she could see inside the car. "Congratulations to all of you," she said. "You can park right where you are," she said. "You're the last to arrive."

Frank turned to Loretta, a question in his eyes.

Loretta sat for a moment, assimilating this new information. She then flashed him the smile that always took his breath away. "Is the bride going to have to open her own car door?"

Frank leapt out and opened her door. The children followed their mother. Mrs. Walters, their beloved babysitter, was waiting at the top of the steps.

"Congratulations, dear," she said, giving Loretta an air kiss on the cheek. Mrs. Walters leaned back and put her hand on Loretta's arm. "I'm so very happy for you." She turned to the children. "We're in the front row." She took Nicole's hand. "Sean—give your arm to Marissa and we'll take our seats. Everyone's waiting."

"Thank you," Loretta said. "Go with Mrs. Walters, and we'll be right behind you."

The town clerk motioned for Frank and Loretta to follow her into the library.

"We'll take care of the marriage license application in here," she said, showing them into the library. David and Glenn Vaughn, each wearing a dark suit adorned with a boutonniere of white roses, flanked the huge fireplace.

Glenn stepped forward, hand outstretched, as they entered the room. "You need two witnesses for a marriage," Glenn said. "And someone has to walk Loretta down the aisle. I hope you don't mind that I volunteered my services when David told me about the wedding."

Loretta nodded, and Frank shook the older man's hand warmly. "We'd be very proud to have you do both."

Glenn turned to Loretta. "You look radiantly beautiful," he said. "Just like a bride should."

The clerk folded the now completed paperwork. "Which one of you gentlemen would like to take charge of this?"

David stepped forward. "I'm the best man," he said, reaching out his hand to take the papers from the clerk.

"All right, then," the clerk said. "Frank, you and David come with me." She turned back to Glenn. "When you hear the wedding march, will you escort our bride to the fireplace in the living room?"

"It would be my honor," Glenn said, holding out his elbow to Loretta.

Loretta slipped her shaking hand into his arm. Glenn patted her hand reassuringly. "It'll be fine," he said softly.

Frank winked at his bride, then followed the clerk and David. He halted abruptly as he stepped into the living room and surveyed a scene he had never imagined would play out in his own life.

The living room furniture had been cleared away, and folding chairs were arranged in rows facing the fireplace. The mantel had been draped in a massive garland of white and cream flowers, matching the swag on the front door. They were identical to the flowers in Loretta's bouquet and his own boutonniere. The woman at the florist's shop must have known about the secret wedding plans when he'd ordered their flowers. Every chair was filled with people he knew. Their faces were turned to his and love and goodwill radiated from every one of them. He blinked hard, struggling to hold back tears. His eyes lighted on Maggie and she nodded and smiled.

The strains of the wedding march came from the piano in the conservatory and Frank moved to the fireplace to await his bride.

The friends and family assembled in the living room rose as Glenn escorted Loretta down the aisle. She was as resplendent in her simple white sheath as she would have been in a designer gown. Her smile lit every corner of the room.

Sam Torres reached over to take Joan's hand, and George and Tonya Holmes exchanged loving glances.

Loretta blew a kiss to her children and took her place opposite her groom in front of the mantel. She lifted her eyes to his and a hush fell over the room. She took his hand and Frank took a step closer to his bride.

The town clerk cleared her throat and the ceremony began.

The brief wedding had been beautiful, and many in attendance were dabbing their eyes as the couple made their way down the aisle.

Judy Young rose from her chair at the back of the room and motioned for the bride and groom to follow her. "We're going to have the receiving line here," she said, leading them to the staircase. "A buffet dinner will be set up on the porch and there are dining tables on the lawn."

Loretta turned wide eyes to Frank. He flushed, and they stepped to the spots Judy indicated.

Loretta's children were the first to approach the newlyweds, followed by Susan and Aaron. "Why don't you join the receiving line?" Susan said, arranging the children next to their mother.

Maggie congratulated the couple. "How in the world?" Frank gasped, taking her hand.

Maggie pulled him to her and hugged him firmly. "You didn't think we'd let you slip off to get married, did you?" She leaned back and looked Frank squarely in the eye. "You're a different person, Frank Haynes. Different than the one I met when I moved here. Everyone in this room loves you, and we wanted you to have a wonderful wedding. And," she said, lowering her voice to a whisper and leaning in, "I think you, of all people, deserve to be married at Rosemont."

Frank nodded, too emotional to trust himself to speak. Maggie began to move away, then turned back to him. "We'd like to invite Sean, Marissa, and Nicole to stay here tonight for a sleepover with Susan. The two of you deserve at least one night of a honeymoon."

Frank beamed as he turned to greet the next person in line.

David turned to Grace as they made their way through the buffet line. "Thank you for coming with me," he said.

"It was fun," Grace said. "This old house is so beautiful, and I love weddings. I just hope it was okay that I came. I didn't want to be a wedding crasher."

"Glenn told me that the best man should bring a date."

Grace blushed. Date. She liked the sound of that. "I've got a ton of homework, so I can't stay late."

"So do I," David replied. "Math?"

Grace nodded. "Want to work on it together tomorrow night? You can stay for supper; my mom always makes extra."

"Sure," David said as they made their way to a small table for two tucked into a corner of the conservatory. "But doing math together isn't my idea of fun. How about we go to a movie Saturday night?"

Grace brightened. "I'd love to."

Glenn caught David's eye as he and Gloria passed through the conservatory on their way to a long table set up on the patio. He gave the lanky youth the thumbs-up sign, and David grinned.

———

Later that evening, Tonya took Frank's outstretched hand and pulled him to her for a hug. "Congratulations, Frank. I'm truly happy for you." She turned to her husband, who was shaking hands with Loretta.

"I hope you have as much happiness in your marriage as Tonya and I have had in ours," George said, nodding to his wife and smiling.

John opened the door to Rosemont, and Tonya and George stepped into the warm evening. The sliver of a moon was hidden behind clouds and fireflies illuminated their path.

"That's the last of the guests," Maggie said.

"We should say goodbye to the kids and get going," Loretta said. She turned to Maggie and tears welled up in her eyes. "Today was absolutely magical. I can't thank you enough for hosting this wedding for us."

"We loved doing it. Judy Young and Joan Torres did most of the work; they're terrific at this sort of thing."

"We'll thank them," Frank interjected. "But Loretta's right. We're very grateful to you, Maggie. This felt like a real wedding, with friends and family all around." His voice choked with emotion. "I never thought I'd marry again, and I certainly didn't think it would be like this."

Maggie stepped to him and put her hand on his arm. "We all found this day very touching, Frank. I hope you now realize that we're all your friends."

Frank shook his head, unable to speak.

Loretta looked at Maggie. "The kids are in the conservatory with Susan and Aaron. They were watching Disney movies, but the last time I checked, they were sound asleep."

"We'll get them into bed. Why don't you leave them be?"

Loretta turned to Frank and nodded. Frank took Loretta's arm and stepped toward the door.

"Before you go," Maggie said, motioning to John, "there's something I want you to have."

John opened the hall closet and pulled out a shimmery white gift bag, tied with an enormous white ribbon. He handed it to Maggie.

"We wanted to give you a piece of Rosemont to start your new life together." She looked at Frank. "You deserve to have this." She placed the bag in Loretta's hands.

Loretta glanced at Frank.

"Open it," Maggie said.

Loretta removed the ribbon and a cloud of white tissue paper, then carefully withdrew a large object swathed in more tissue, taped into place. She handed the object to Frank while she pulled off the pieces of tape.

Loretta gasped as the last piece of tissue fell aside to reveal a graceful silver water pitcher. The handle was generously carved, but the bowl of the pitcher was simple and unadorned. Loretta held it up to the light to admire it. "It's beautiful, Maggie." She handed the pitcher to Frank and hugged her. "Thank you."

Frank turned the pitcher over in his hands. "This is old, isn't it?"

"Yes," Maggie replied. "It was in the butler's pantry. It was horribly tarnished, but we cleaned it up and it's quite presentable now."

"I'll say," Frank replied.

Maggie slipped her arm around John's waist. "We've been so happy here. I hope it brings you good luck."

"I have a feeling it will," Frank said. He pulled the massive mahogany door open. He and Loretta joined hands and made their way to their car. John and Maggie stepped onto the driveway and waved until the taillights were out of sight.

Chapter 44

Maggie smiled at the lanky figure striding down the back lawn at Rosemont. She started to rise from her perch on the low stone wall, but he motioned for her to stay put.

"I suspected I'd find you out here drinking your morning cup of coffee," Alex said. "I remember that was your habit when Marc and I lived with you after our accident."

Maggie patted the spot on the wall next to her. "The morning light on the rear facade of Rosemont is beautiful, don't you think? The mullioned windows sparkle like diamonds."

Alex leaned against the wall and turned back to look at the house. "You're right. It's also substantial and comforting. Timeless. No matter what's going on in your life, Rosemont will be here."

"Exactly." Maggie turned to him. "You just missed Susan and Aaron. They left to drop Loretta's kids off at school and then they're going to Tim's office to sign papers."

"I was coming to see you, actually. Your assistant said you don't plan to be in the office until after lunch." He paused and took a deep breath. "It's all coming together, isn't it?"

"It appears so. We've finally got the crooks who committed the embezzlement and fraud, Susan and Aaron are settling in Westbury to raise their family, and Loretta and Frank are married. If you'd have told me all this six months ago, I'd never have believed it."

"How was the wedding?" Alex asked.

"It was lovely," Maggie said. "I think they're going to make each other very happy. I'm sorry you missed it." She raised an eyebrow at him quizzically.

"You'll be glad to hear what I was doing instead," Alex said. "I was finalizing Frank's plea deal with his lawyer and the judge."

Maggie turned to face him. "And?"

"Frank will get a seven-year sentence—all of it suspended."

Maggie released the breath she had been holding. "No jail time. Thank goodness."

Alex nodded. "He'll pay a fine of one and a half million dollars and will be sentenced to perform three thousand hours of community service."

"That seems steep."

"He readily agreed to it."

"Anything else?" Maggie asked.

"Tim Knudsen suggested that Frank serve his community service time as a consultant to the group working to restore the pension fund. Tim is chairman of that group and feels Frank's business acumen will be extremely useful."

Maggie considered this. "That makes sense. Tim told me the other day that the properties owned by the pension fund may be more valuable than they originally thought. He feels that careful management of those properties will go a long way toward restoring stability to the fund. I can see how Frank's advice would be beneficial."

"You really believe Frank's turned over a new leaf, don't you?"

Maggie shook her head emphatically.

"I'll keep an open mind on the issue." He smiled at her.

"That's all anyone could ask for."

"I didn't stop by just to tell you about Frank's plea deal. I wanted to let you know that I'll be moving my office out of Town Hall and back to my law firm."

"Why?"

"Now that most of the loose ends of the case are tied up, there's really nothing for a special counsel to do."

"What about rebuilding Town Hall?"

"That's a job for the mayor." He smiled at her. "As much as I've loved working at Town Hall, you don't need me anymore."

"Isn't it about time you became mayor?" Maggie asked. "Would you be interested if the job were available?"

One look at his face gave her his answer.

"I'd never run against you," Alex replied.

Maggie smiled and rested her hand on his arm. "You wouldn't have to. Let me tell you about my next chapter …"

The End

Thank You for Reading!

If you enjoyed *Bringing Them Home*, I'd be grateful if you wrote a review.

Just a few lines would be great. Reviews are the best gift an author can receive. They encourage us when they're good, help us improve our next book when they're not, and help other readers make informed choices when purchasing books. Reviews keep the Amazon algorithms humming and are the most helpful aide in selling books! Thank you.

To post a review on Amazon or for Kindle:

1. Go to the product detail page for *Bringing Them Home* on Amazon.com.
2. Click "Write a customer review" in the Customer Reviews section.
3. Write your review and click Submit.

In gratitude,

Barbara Hinske

Just for You!

Wonder what Maggie was thinking when the book ended? Exclusively for readers who finished *Bringing Them Home*, take a look at Maggie's Diary Entry for that day at https://barbarahinske.com/maggies-diary.

Acknowledgements

I'm blessed with the wisdom and support of many kind and generous people. I want to thank the most supportive and delightful group of champions an author could hope for:

My incredibly patient and supportive husband, Brian;

My beta reader and book guru, Helen Curl;

My genius marketing team of Mitch Gandy, Jesse Doubek, and Jill Bates Wallace—thank you for always fueling my dreams;

My kind and generous attorney, Roger A. Grad;

The professional "dream team" of my editors Linden Gross and Jesika St. Clair, life coach Mat Boggs, and author assistant Lisa Coleman;

Matt Hinrichs for another beautiful cover; and

The Tooms family for generously allowing me to use their Texie as my Eve.

Book Club Questions

**(If your club talks about anything other than
family, jobs, and household projects!)**

1. Do you have a pet? What kind and why did you choose it?
2. What benefits or blessings do you experience from owning a pet?
3. Do you have a therapy dog or have you ever seen one in action?
4. Have you ever had an encore career? What was it?
5. What prompted you to change careers?
6. If you could have another career now, what would it be?
7. What activities would you like to spend more time doing?
8. What would you like to spend less time doing?
9. What is the most influential piece of advice you've ever received?
10. What would you say to a group of graduates?

About the Author

Barbara Hinske is an attorney by day, bestselling novelist by night. She inherited the writing gene from her father who wrote mysteries when he retired and told her a story every night of her childhood. She and her husband share their own Rosemont with two adorable and spoiled dogs. The old house keeps her husband busy with repair projects and her happily decorating, entertaining, cooking, and gardening. Together they have four grown children, and live in Phoenix, Arizona.

Please enjoy this chapter from

The Christmas Club

The Barbara Hinske book readers are hailing as "heartwarming,"
"uplifting," and "an instant holiday classic"

The heavy revolving door picked up speed, knocking Verna Lind's gloves
out of her hand and flinging her from the warmth of the Cleveland bank
into the frigid December air. Despite the flat soles of her sensible work
shoes, her left foot slipped on the icy pavement, and both she and her large
purse came crashing down. The purse's well-worn metal clasp burst open,
spilling her possessions across the walk and into West Third Street. Dazed,
Verna blinked and began to crawl toward the smattering of five-dollar bills
lying in the road when a sudden gust of wind lifted her Christmas savings
and sent it soaring into traffic.

———

Edward Fuller bent his lanky frame into the wind as he dashed down West
Third Street, one hand gripping the tan fedora on his head, the other carrying a heavy briefcase. His oral argument before the court had gone well. If
he hurried, he'd have time to get something to eat before his next client
appointment at two thirty. He hated missing lunch. Being a bachelor, that
was his only decent meal of the day.

Edward skirted the mob of people flooding from the bank's revolving
door, which was in constant motion this time of year. He was almost past
the exit when he saw an elderly woman burst through the door, arms flail-
ing wildly before she tumbled to her knees. A man followed on her heels,
stepped over her without offering assistance, and hurried off.

Edward pushed through the crowd to reach the woman sprawled on the
ground. "Ma'am," he said, setting his briefcase on the sidewalk and squat-
ting down next to her as she tried to get up. "Are you all right?"

Verna nodded. "I've got to get my money." She turned to him as her
eyes filled with tears. "That's my Christmas money. I've saved all year. I've
got to get it back."

Edward adjusted his heavy black glasses and stared. *Surely she knew that
her money was gone?*

"If you haven't hurt yourself, let's help you get inside the bank," came a woman's voice over his shoulder. An easy-on-the-eyes brunette dressed in a bright red coat with fur collar and cuffs leaned over him and looked anxiously at the woman.

Verna shook her head. "I've got to get it ..."

"We'll help you inside, then we'll come back outside to look for your money," the young woman insisted, placing an arm under Verna's elbow and motioning for Edward to do the same. Together, they helped Verna to her feet and escorted her back through the revolving door. They crossed the bank's lobby to a group of straight backed chairs along the wall, the young woman's high heels tapping out a staccato rhythm on the marble floor as they made their way. Verna sank into a chair without further protest.

"I'll go look for your money," Edward said. "How much did you have?"

"Thirty dollars. All in fives," Verna said. "A year's worth of savings." She shook her head. "There's no way you'll find it. It'll be long gone by now."

"You don't know that," he said. "I'm at least going to try."

"I'll find someone to bring you some water. Then I'll go help him," the young woman said, gesturing to Edward as he exited the lobby. "Will you be all right here on your own?"

Verna nodded.

"Don't leave until we come back," the young woman said before catching the eye of a banker crossing the lobby. "This woman fell in your doorway," she said. "Would you please bring her a glass of water?"

"Of course," he said, eying Verna with concern. "Should I call a doctor?"

"No, thank you. I'll just wait here until my friends return," Verna said, directing a thin smile at the young woman.

Clad in her red coat, the woman emerged from the revolving door of the bank looking like she'd stepped from the pages of a fashion magazine. Edward Fuller stood stock still, taking in the determined set of her shoulders and the graceful curves of her profile. His internal compass responded to her as if she were true north. He would later confess that was the moment. The moment that he knew—Carol Clark was "the one."

She turned her head left and then right, searching for him. He held up his hand, and she flashed *that smile*. He shook his head, and she joined him on the sidewalk.

"Nothing? What a shame," she said. "Seems like an old dear. Still working, I'd say. By the looks of her shoes, I'd guess that she's on her feet all day." She looked into Edward's eyes. "I'm heartbroken for her."

Edward nodded and pushed his glasses up on his nose. "I've had an idea, though. I've got five five-dollar bills in my wallet. I thought I'd give them to her."

"That's terribly kind of you, but I don't think she'll want your charity."

"I don't plan to tell her it's from me. I'll say we found it on the street. Tucked into the corner of a building or something. I know that will leave her five dollars short. I'd be happy to give it to her in ones, but I agree with you—I don't think she'll take it."

She smiled again and the temperature suddenly felt twenty degrees warmer to him. "I have a five in my purse," she replied. "What a nice thing for you to do. I'd be happy to contribute." She retrieved the bill from her wallet and handed it to him.

"I'm Carol Clark," she said, extending her hand once more. Edward took her hand in his own. It was warm and smooth and her handshake, firm and definite.

"Edward Fuller."

"What a lovely little Christmas secret we'll share, Edward Fuller," she said. "Let's go back in there and make that sweet lady very happy."

———

Verna patted the thick mass of graying blond hair secured in a bun at the nape of her neck and took a sip of her water, all the while keeping her aquamarine eyes trained on the revolving glass door. Her feet ached—as they always did after her shift at the bakery—and she was glad for the chance to sit down. She'd been sending up silent prayers that the two young people who came to her rescue would find her money—her Christmas money. It was December 15, and she'd just withdrawn all the money she'd saved in her Christmas club account.

She smiled to herself as she thought of the amount she'd been able to put aside this year. More customers were depositing their pennies and nickels in the tip jar on the counter. The attorney who came in every morning for two glazed doughnuts left a whole dollar every Friday. The economy in 1952 was booming; all the papers said so. Verna had been able to save most of her share of the tips. And she'd had thirty dollars to prove it. *Imagine that.* Eight dollars more than she'd been able to save last year. Everyone on her list would get something nice. She had next Monday off, and she'd do all of her shopping then—assuming the strangers who had stopped to help her found the bills the wind had swept away.

As the minutes ticked by, she became increasingly anxious. Asking God to help with this small request was a waste of His time. She ought to be ashamed of herself for asking Him. Verna looked at the large clock on the opposite wall. These young people were undoubtedly employed somewhere nearby and had probably already gone back to work. She'd wait another few minutes, then be on her way.

A flash of red in the revolving door caught Verna's eye before the beautiful Carol Clark stepped into the lobby. Edward Fuller was on her heels. The looks on their faces made Verna's heart race. Maybe, just maybe, her prayers had been answered. She put her hands on the arms of the chair and began to rise, but Carol motioned her to sit.

"He's found it!" she cried. "All of it! Isn't he brilliant?"

"What?" Verna gasped. "I never in a million years thought I'd see all of it again. How far did you have to look?"

"Not far, as it turns out." Edward concocted a story on the spot. "It had all gotten caught underneath a trash can across the street, where it was protected from the wind. This must be your lucky day," he said, handing her the neatly folded stack of bills.

Verna took them from his hand and opened her purse, zipping them safely into a side compartment. "I'm not taking any chances," she said, snapping the purse shut and tilting her head to smile up at them. "Thank you for taking the time to assist an old lady."

"We were glad we could help," Carol said. "You really owe it all to Mr. Fuller's quick action."

"I'm so grateful," Verna patted Edward's arm. "And now, I'd better let you two be on your way."

Edward extended his hand and helped her to her feet. "Where are you headed?" he asked.

"Home," she replied. "My bus should be along any minute."

"Let me help you to your bus stop," he said as the three of them traversed the lobby and made a slow exit out of the revolving door.

"It's just down the block, there," Verna said, pointing to a group of people waiting by the curb. She looked from one to the other. "Thank you, again, for your kindness to me. You've been my Christmas miracle. I'll put you in my prayers. And a very blessed Christmas to you both." With that, she set out for the bus stop.

Edward and Carol stood together on the pavement, watching Verna walk away. Carol turned to face him and waited.

Edward cleared his throat. "Well, Miss Clark. Very nice to meet you. Have a good afternoon."

She smiled and something flashed behind her eyes. Was it disappointment? "You too, Mr. Fuller. And a very merry Christmas."

He tipped his hat, and Carol turned and walked away. Edward checked his watch. He no longer had time for lunch and was already late for his next appointment. He set out for his office at a brisk pace, berating himself with each step. *Why hadn't he asked her out to dinner? Or at least gotten her phone number or found out where she worked?* It had been years since anyone had turned his head; he was sorely out of practice.

Edward cursed under his breath and forced his way back through the throng of people he'd just passed, retracing his steps. His long strides ate up the pavement, and his height allowed him a clear view of the other pedestrians. After three blocks he was forced to admit that he'd lost her. He slapped his thigh with his gloved hand and stomped his foot, ignoring the curious glances from passersby. *Why in the hell had he been so slow—so stupid?* If there really were Christmas miracles, maybe he would see Carol Clark again.

Available at Amazon
and for Kindle

Novels in the *Rosemont* series

Coming to Rosemont
Weaving the Strands
Uncovering Secrets
Drawing Close
Bringing Them Home

Also by BARBARA HINSKE

The Night Train
The Christmas Club

I'd love to hear from you!

Connect with me online:

Visit **www.barbarahinske.com** to
sign up for my **newsletter** to receive your Free Gift,
plus Inside Scoops, Amazing Offers,
Bedtime Stories & Inspirations from Home.

Facebook.com/BHinske
Twitter.com/BarbaraHinske
Email me at **bhinske@gmail.com**

Search for **Barbara Hinske on YouTube**
for tours inside my own historic
home plus tips and tricks for busy women!

Find photos of fictional *Rosemont*, Westbury,
and things related to the *Rosemont*
series at **Pinterest.com/BarbaraHinske**.

Made in the USA
Lexington, KY
26 May 2017